Letters from the Karst

JANE OLMSTED

Legacy Book Press LLC
Camanche, Iowa

For my children and grandchildren, those who live and those who died, and for those who have not yet come along.

And for Teresa Christmas, artist, teacher, and friend—for all you give to our community, and to me.

Acknowledgements

I started writing about this family more than twenty years ago and have "finished" it many times. Each time I put it away, tucked in a folder on my laptop, the Collins family and the people they touched talked with each other and eventually let me know that they were still waiting on me to bring them into the outer world. Each time I opened that door (clicked on that folder) I saw again how much I liked them, how their stories help me tell my own story, a love story, really, about Kentucky and about the wounds that shape us. A different kind of cave features in each story or chapter; like the caves, they are connected both intimately and co-incidentally. I am grateful to members of my family, friends, colleagues, students, neighbors who were the inspiration for the characters in *Letters from the Karst*. And I'm grateful they kept calling out from that vast internal landscape, pulling me back to their world (which is also our world).

Table of Contents

Letters from the Karst..1

My Silver Bowl..17

Early Blur...34

Abandoned Quarry 47

Don't Say Maybe..62

Achers Pond 80

Who Do You Love? 99

Lost River 105

Movie Lines..121

On the Beautiful O-hi-o..136

Etremophiles 150

About the Author...163

Artist's Statement 165

Letters from the Karst

Dear Mom,

I've received your letters and want you to know that I appreciate what you're trying to do, but I'm not coming home for Christmas, so you can call off the letter writing campaign before anyone gets a cramp for nothing.

You want to know what I'm thinking about these days. It's pretty boring in here. I'm not up on current events, and fashion stinks. If you're looking for intellectual stimulation, then I'm a hole you don't want to stumble into. Think of me as a mammoth cave. Your letters just flutter through the stale air, talk echoes; memories suffocate. A year ago people used to have dark circles where there should be faces, but now I see their noses plain as day. Doesn't that convince you that I'm making progress and maybe it's *because* I'm on my own?

You've always been there to bail me out, so I've made a sacred promise that I won't come home until I have patched myself back together. I crossed my heart and hoped to die, stuck a needle in my eye, cut both my index fingers, and pressed the drops of blood together. You wouldn't want me to go back on a promise, would you?

Try thinking of me as a distant relation.

Cecily

There were eight of them in all, including the one I wrote and my mother's two. I found them when we were cleaning out my old bedroom, where they were stored in a box of papers marked "Cecily: 1990-2000" (more years than any other box, but then look at all that dead space). I knew what they were right away and slipped them into my bag while Mom's back was turned. They're mine, after all, even if I left them here last year when I moved into my tiny apartment and realized that "setting up housekeeping," as Grandma calls it, didn't mean I had to take every scrap of paper that had my name on it.

"Read me," they say.

They are what my therapist Jeannine calls my litmus test. Storing them where 40 years from now they can come back to haunt me—that takes a lot of faith, she says, and that's what I need. Read them every so often, she suggested. Some people prove themselves bouncing at the end of a rubber cord and some of us curled up in a favorite chair, trying not to watch the minute hand drag its late self to the next tock. Hitting rock bottom is about as good a term as any. You're either alone or sharing the pits with a few other losers, and way far away on the brink, you can see your family and friends from before. If you're lucky, when they turn their backs to walk away, they don't wave. And for the rest of your life you're picking bits of glass and shale out of your face and butt.

I can't blame anyone—no one mistreated me. I wasn't deserted. I was loved. I am loved. It was an accident. First, I was fourteen and partying on week-ends with some older kids. Shooting tequila, swallowing skittles. Then fifteen and smoking pot before school, skipping school, and driving to Nashville with other party kids where we'd shoplift till we poured into a booth and started cutting lines with my school ID. I sat across from my boyfriend's cousin and watched his sinuses spill out of his left nostril, along with white-flaked blood. I was scared but when he didn't die, I thought I'd dreamt it. I've been busted twice. When the Butler County meth lab blew and almost took me with it, I was seventeen and ready to surrender.

My mother had been writing since I left Ten Broeck Psychiatric Hospital and moved into the transitional home with three others. Her letters, at least before this bundle, were light, full of stories about the family, what she was doing, silly things at work. I read them quickly and then threw them out. Even though she's the reason I'm alive, that shadow of disappointment was all it would take to crack my eggshell life—I could touch the inside of that oval and feel how thin it was.

All the king's horses, all the king's men . . .

Dear Cecily,

I won't try to address all you said in your letter just yet, but I do want you to know that the "letter writing campaign," as you call it, is out of my hands. All I did was mention that you might be persuaded to come home for Christmas now that you're out of the program, and since we don't know where you're staying in Louisville (and no one would violate your wishes and try to find you), your sister suggested we all write letters "the old fashioned way."

Notice I didn't say which sister, so it may surprise you that it was Molly.

As if any of your family could ever consider you a distant relation, or a cave, for godssake. . . . But okay, I'll try to go with that one for the sake of argument, but if you're going to be a mammoth cave then are you sure that space you describe is empty? Mammoth Cave is not a lone crack in the world's surface but a network of living spaces, inhabited by rare and beautiful treasures. If you are a cave, then you are a place so profound it strikes awe in my heart, so tenuous that caution springs to my lips—please, passerby, be careful. She is strong but not invincible. She can be polluted. She is lovely but not safe.

As far as bailing goes, you're not the only one with promises to keep. I hope you will reconsider and come home to visit. We won't over-shower you with kisses. You always loved the Christmas Eve service. For me, clever cave, the greatest gift would be to see you again.

Love, Mom

Uncle Ned. He was my favorite person when I was a kid, big and gentle as a panda, but prone to impatience. His wife, Lilly, left him when I was just getting started, for a childhood sweetheart, and Ned and Sonny followed her to Ohio. He tried to win her back but it didn't work. A lonely man, I realized the other day, though it's probably been obvious to everyone else for years. How do you find a new mate in a small town, when you live and hunt alone?

Sonny, the cousin who hung out with us girls most of his life, is now almost finished with his degree in engineering, which he loves because it allows him to make his meticulous drawings and imagine bridges spanning enormous spaces.

Cecily,

Aunt Meredith says we should all write to you at your secret PO, and Bossy Mossy gave us two rules. We're not allowed to say mean things about you, and we're sposd to talk about how we're doing, and tell you something we remember about you. That sounds like 3 rules. I remember you used to always say, "2+2 doesn't always equal 4." By us doing this you will want to come home and find out what's really going on. So okay, I'm down.

What jumps into my head right now is when me and Dad came back from Ohio after our year in hell. I couldn't connect with my old friends, but you were so cool—you must have been about 15, since I know I was 13. Molly used to grab my hand and haul me around. "Come on, Sonny, let's go pick some strawburries and make strawburry milkshakes." You were working at DQ and always going out on weekends, but after school we'd go to your grandma's barn, throw saddles on the horses, and go riding till dinner, and before it got cold, stop at the pond and lay around on the raft. We had the most grownup conversations, seemed like, and having such a popular girl spending time with me, well, I don't care if it sounds pathetic because coming home was easier because of you.

Really, Cousin Cess, you're my fav. I don't care how bad off you've been, you're still the prettiest and smartest and the most fun to smartaleck around with. And Iago misses you.

Yours in disaster, Sonny

Cecily,

I told Meredith that I didn't think this business of writing letters would do anything but set your jaw, but she just gave me "the look." Who knows, maybe your sisters can get through.

You couldn't have done a better job if you'd lined them up like a row of sitting ducks.

Diana. Forge her signature. Drain her savings account. *Pching.* Laugh at your grandmother's art. *Pching.*

I don't want to know the cannon you used on Molly.

And your mother's still clutching her heart.

Sonny and I were lucky, just a little collateral damage.

She showed me the letter you wrote. I like the bit about the promise you made yourself, the only part that rang true in that whole self-centered letter. I can see you doing the blood brother thing with yourself. Blood sister, whatever. Always the one for rituals.

Like the time you insisted on a funeral service for Rusty. Even if he was the best hound ever, it was a little over the top. Still, I was touched. You handing me the handful of dirt to throw over the top of the grave you'd prepared. "Come on, Uncle Ned, sprinkle it, like this," then showing me with your own handful, and later asking, "Why do they do that with the dirt?"

You can tear a person up and never blink.

Or maybe I'm just too dense to see what you were trying to say, with that business about the cave. Distant relation. There's no such thing. I guess you're just going to have to explain it to me in person. I'd like to see what your eyes are doing when you tell it.

Well, I don't want to close like this, so I'll tell you what I can see clearly, and it goes all the way back to when you were two months old and your mother set you in my arms so she could go be sick—some virus she had. Up to that point I had no interest in children, let alone babies. I was sure I'd drop you. "Get over yourself," she said as she thrust you at me. You stared at me and squirmed a little like you weren't too comfortable. Started to cry. I picked up a bottle with my free hand and leveled it at you. That did the trick and you grasped my pinky with one hand, squeezing it like you were keeping rhythm to the sucking. I lost track of time, lost in those deep blue eyes that seemed to see something in mine. Then you gave a big sigh and smiled, that nipple still plugged into the roof of your mouth.

What a rush of something. I have you to thank for Sonny, in a way, since it wasn't till that moment that it ever occurred to me that I could be a father, let alone enjoy it. Your mother found me that way, almost blubbering. I can see now when it was that this boy became a man, and what a wee thing it was who did it. I'm saying that I guess you can do whatever you set your mind to, including make a liar out of me.

Be seeing you, Uncle Ned

My grandmother was a painter who taught high school art her whole life. Lately, her canvases have been tiny, the smallest about two inches square and the largest the size of a plate. She has one brush with sable hairs like a thread. The other day I stood in front of a series of three she's got hanging in the hall, each one the face of a cube, each block more raised than the previous. "Steppingstones: splish . . . splash . . . space." Splish is an almost flat cube of swirling white and green around a spot of gray that you can only see when you don't look directly at it—water. Splash rises almost an inch, is darker, more swirl, and the gray spot has disappeared—deeper water. And space—almost two inches rising, and the colors have lifted as well, the paint globular, greens and purples, the swirling stopped, layering almost. "It's simple," she said when I asked her. "It's stumble-fall-leap. I made them for you."

Dear One,

Meredith shared your letter with me, and though I'd already bought this card and written on it, I now have something more to say. Since you were a child, I have watched you attack life, retire from it, swing back and hit it with all your might, crumble, get up, hit it again, fall, rise, fall, and rise again. You take things personally, when in fact sometimes s—t just happens.

I want to talk to you about yourself by talking about others, two others to be exact.

So first, your father. David was such an exciting young man, and Meredith and he just radiated when they were together. Oh, the hours they'd spend on the phone whenever Meredith came home during school breaks. Me having to hear just one side of it, or not even that, but the sound of one side of it, the quality of voice, breathless, bubbling, intimate. And it didn't let up the way it does for so many people, not as I ever saw, right through the years of schooling, one degree after another. Books and babies. Meredith nursing you kids in one hand and holding a book in the other. David typing, his legs shaking nervously, which would put you sprawled across his lap to sleep. I never knew how.

The two of them, with their Ph.Ds. and their book publications, conferences, guest lecturing, students coming by the house . . . Well, that public image of his belied a very troubled man. After he was diagnosed, not till well into his thirties as bi-polar, he refused medication. Since his mood swings were unpredictable, and there might be long periods when he seemed normal, it was easy for him, and your mother, to believe that the latest manic period was the last. But experience taught us to recognize the slide—it was like slipping—starting with restlessness then a heightened state of creativity and intense intellectual work that he tried to make last as long as he could. This was when he got most of his best work done. But it never failed that after the paper or the chapter or the book was written, he would plummet. And that's when you girls learned to give him a wider berth.

When he died, you three were 5, 8, and 12. Meredith worried about him, up till 4 a.m. writing his last book. His eyes were red-rimmed and there was a peculiar smell about him—like sweat but sharper, almost like an electrical fire behind the wall. Maybe I imagined that. Your mom tried to get him to rest, to accept massages, calming teas, anything short of going to the doctor, which he would not allow. When I dropped you girls off that day—you'd been out to the farm all day and were so deliriously happy and exhausted—you crawled willingly, after your baths, into bed, even though it was well before bedtime.

Your father was making himself a cocktail—probably his second or even third, his hand slipped somehow, and he cut his finger, slicing it down to the bone. Meredith and I ran into the kitchen to see him clutching his hand with a bloody towel. "I'll run to the hospital and get it stitched," he said, "Don't come with me." And that's how he left. You see, your father wrapped that car around a tree because he refused help. Barely a quarter mile up the road! Not on purpose, but he was no longer in the driver's seat, not the real David, who loved you girls more than anything in the world, loved his wife, a dynamic teacher, but some troubled version, his nerves shot, someone *beside himself.* And he would have welcomed some help, if he'd had a chance to rewrite that day, like one of his poems, with a different ending. You are your father's daughter.

But you are also your mother's.

And this is the second person I want to talk to you about, even at the risk of telling you what you already know. If that's the case, just remember how old I am. But I want to tell you what I suspect no one has told you about last Christmas, when you were taken away.

It was Christmas Eve day that your mother returned alone from Rivendell, after seeing you delivered into the hands of the escort from Louisville, where you would spend the next six months at that hospital. I was with your sisters, and Sonny and Uncle Ned were here as well. We were all pretty shaken, but we went ahead with decorating the tree. I heard your mother's car pull in the driveway, and when she didn't come into the living room, after a time I went to the kitchen to find her.

She sat at the kitchen table, her chair pulled back from it, her arms dangling at her sides, her head hung over, and her hair falling forward. "Meredith," I started. Her voice was barely audible. "Don't, don't," she said, so I stopped and stood back, waiting for her to make the next move. Who knows how long I might have waited had not your sisters, Sonny, and Ned followed me. All you could hear were the sniffles of your sisters. Now, you may think this next part is grandstanding, but it's where you and your mother are most alike. For both of you, it's always been important that certain things, call them life's transitions, be done right. She finally looked up and said, "Cecily will be gone now for six months, and we must hope for the best. You may do as you like, but I will not be speaking again until New Year's Day. This is my prayer, for my daughter whom I love." Her voice cracked on the word love. Molly flung her arms around her waist and buried her head in her lap. Diana followed and stood behind her, hugging her shoulders and resting her cheek on her head. And then Sonny went and took her right hand. Neddy followed and took her left. And it seemed that all her family had claimed some piece of her body (you at the very center), and it was left to me to somehow take everybody in my arms, which I tried to do.

It's time for you to come home and claim your spot in this family's tableau.

Your loving grandmother

Two letters are from my sisters, Molly and Diana. Both rock solid next to my hill of shale, sturdy eggs to my Humpty Dumpty. Diana in law school, Molly about to graduate from high school, bound for, of course, Western Kentucky University, where Mom teaches, where Dad taught, where Sonny and Diana went to school, everyone marching through. I look in one direction and see Diana, her spiked hair, her sense of right and wrong, and know she'll be such a good civil rights lawyer. It probably doesn't hurt that she loves to win. When I was in middle school and she was in high school, I stopped playing any kind of game with her. I was happy to let her win, and that just made her mad. On my other side is Molly. Put her on a horse and she's in her domain— and so is the horse. All my life, Diana on my right, and Molly, once she was born, on my left, given to me when I turned three as my surprise birthday present. But, wait. I'm like one of these memory boxes, as Mom calls them, which trace only the high points—our awards, birthday cards, pictures in the newspaper or school newsletters, the steppingstones, in a way, that mark our successes, our happy moments.

Dear Cecily,

This is a lot harder than I thought it would be. I've already thrown the first 8 tries away, and so I'm just going to write without stopping and shove it in an envelope without looking, forgive the mistakes. And then I'm going to go watch *Buffy.*

You would not recognize me. I'm 15 years old now, which happened ten months ago, in case you forgot when my birthday is, ha ha. When you left before last Christmas, we were the bitterest of enemies. I really hated you for trying to ruin my family, including moi. You used to at least pretend to care until you got on the crackwagon and tried to trick me into dating your pimp when I was only 13. Mom wouldn't be so keen on that little piece of Cecily history, do you think? But I'm not like you, I keep things that are HURTFUL to myself.

When you try to take people down with you, there are going to be hard feelings. Mom made me go to a therapist, and it turned out to be pretty good. I was in a group that met every week, and even though I'm not a recovering addict, this group is for teens with family members who are. Some of them it's just a matter of time, I can tell, but other kids were really brave and went through a lot rougher things than I ever did, and they will never never do what their mother or father or aunt or uncle or in one case brother did to them.

So, one thing they kept drilling us about is that substance abuse is a disease and that everyone who makes it easier for the addict ("call it what it is") has it too. What I want to say is, oh boy I can't believe I'm going to put this on paper, I really do love you and want my big sister back. I keep remembering when you were still a human being who happened to care about me. You'll also be surprised when I tell you that it was my big fat idea to write letters to you, so it's up to me to get it all out, since it's been a year since we've been within spitting distance and even longer since I wished you were dead.

So last week I started looking through the photo albums from when we were all younger and I pulled out two. The first is of you and me with Iago and Babe on my 10th birthday. Our two horses are standing on either side of us and you have your arm around me and we're both smiling and Iago's looking bored and Babe is pulling at the bit. You have this big smile on your face and so do I, and that's where I can see that we're sisters, even though my teeth are crooked (and buck like Bugs). And things were really good for about a year, weren't they? We'd go riding just about every weekend.

I like to make the sour memories disappear and then it's just me and you riding through the woods, talking about grownup things, and then racing the last half mile home. Then we'd rub them down and it would be just the horse sounds and smells. Remember my poster? "Happiness is" at the top, and at the bottom, "a girl and her Arabian" with a picture in the middle of me cantering Babe towards the camera. That's the second picture, even though you're not in it, you're behind it. Best Christmas present ever, thank you Cecily. When I look at that first picture I can feel the weight of your arm around my neck. And with the second, I can hear you say, "Molly, for chrissake, don't run me down."

If you come home, I won't steal your cigarettes, like I use to, or whatever else I could find that not having it would cause you grief. And we can visit Babe and Iago (Sonny's been riding him some, even though he's kinda lame).

Your sister, Molly

Dear Sissy,

When we met in Louisville and I saw how you've changed, I drove all the way home thinking that I had to tell Mom, that it wasn't fair to keep it a secret. I haven't told her . . . and every day that passes it gets harder. I wish I'd broken my promise and told her that night.

I sure played the big sister card. How many times did I say "you should" in that two-hour meeting in Cherokee Park? And you whispering, "I know" and "I know, you're right," each time your voice lower and more discouraged. I guess the pep talk was more a letdown talk, wasn't it. And I've been feeling bad, really bad that I couldn't just listen. How did I become the preachy di-ann landers of this family!

I wouldn't blame you if you went back to your housemates and laughed it up after I left. "Hey, Edna, do you know what my sister said?" "No, we cannot imagine." "She said, 'Maybe if you could get your hair styled and wear something that makes you feel real good about yourself, you wouldn't slouch so.'" And then Edna, "Well at least she didn't suggest you quit smoking."

Hah! Ugh, I'm just shuddering.

I think that's why I never told Mom. Even if I could have left out me telling you how to live something like my life, I would have looked like a liar, guilt on my face like egg. Will you ever be able to help me laugh this off? The way you used to wipe away my blues, my little sister, so much better at being the big sister than the big sister. At least before IT.

I can't bear another silent Christmas, Cecily, without us in our pajamas (oversized tee and boxers for you). You making coffee and me making Bisquick coffee cake. Molly squeezing the oranges. Mom helping Grandma down the stairs. Sonny and Ned on their way. Molly insisting on Raffi's Christmas CD, and you and me secretly enjoying it, rolling our eyes to "On Christmas morning, we can sing and celebrate, and make the feeling last all through the year."

Last year was the first year we weren't together. I mean there've been years when other people have been with us. Dad at the beginning. Aunt Lilly. Grandpa. But last year's Christmas was the saddest ever. Mom just awash in sobless tears and all of us feeling helpless. Molly with her rage, saying to Mom, "Go ahead, wallow in it if you want, but I'm glad she's gone!" Grandma turning away, "Oh, Molly, how could you." Molly firing back, "Can it, old bitch," then racing up the stairs, to cry in private. The gifts sitting there for a week before anyone would open them—except Molly, who defiantly opened hers, with loud commentary: "Oh, how lovely, you shouldn't have." "Just what I always wanted, a jewelry box, oh what a clever girl." How I wanted to smack her! Warning look from Mom. (Later when Mom went for a walk we did come to blows and Uncle Ned had to pull us a part, just like he used to when we were all brats, a handful of hair in her fist, a pound of her flesh under my fingernails, and poor Sonny wringing his hands, and Uncle Ned saying, "I've a mind to switch you both.") Finally, in the evening a sullen ride around town to look at the lights, ho ho ho.

You said you don't remember last Christmas, but you'll remember this one. You're back among the living, Sissy, and there's no denying it.

Ever your (older) sister, Diana

I stand up, fluff the pillow. Light another cigarette.

Dear Family,

You really know how to get to a girl. I've been crying for three days, reading your letters.

What can I say?

There's nothing to say.

How can I face you, I don't think I can.

You're all so strong, I'll be blown away. Pulverized.

I just can't do it. I'm sorry. Truly I am.

I'm so ashamed and so afraid.

What if I lose everything I've gained over the past year?

I love you. Forgive me.

Cecily

Dearest Daughter,

I am coming to Louisville. Molly and Diana are coming with me, December 23. We'll leave at 9:00, 10:00 your time, which will put us at the playground in Cherokee Park—Diana says you'll know where we mean—between noon and 12:30.

I should like to talk with you about the word "pulverize": to disintegrate, demolish. It sounds like something that happens quickly, but it is a process. It sounds like a machine that turns to grit whatever it's fed. A greedy mouth. An unforgiving mouth.

It is part of another process I should like you to think about. It is a cave process. It is infinitely patient. Or maybe outside of patience. A relentless creativity, let's say. The cave reaches out of itself in countless directions, creating—or finding—waterways and air passages, some so tiny that you don't realize that you have felt its breath, a thing so slight you must doubt its existence. Sometimes the cave traps poisonous fumes. Sometimes the cave saves living creatures when the cold outside would kill them. Some living things—blind shrimp, for instance—are found nowhere else on earth. Moisture rich with minerals gathers at the ceilings and on the floors, building up, building down. Stalactites, you used to say, "because they hold on *tight*." And stalagmites, "because they *might* make it to the top!"

We are all of us caves, my girl. We grow up, we grow down. Some caves are deeper than others, but all of us have depths we have yet to plumb. You are part of a karst system bigger than yourself. Pack a bag of whatever you want to bring with you.

It's your choice, Cecily. . . . XX

It was a mild but windy day when I had Edna drop me off at 11:45. I wanted to be there before they arrived so I could watch them, make up my mind.

"You sure you don't want me to stay?"

"I'm sure. If you don't see me, I'll call you next week, okay?"

Edna's from eastern Kentucky, almost done getting her teeth replaced after a life of disregard. She's a great imitator of her favorite shows—the local news, Martha Stewart, and Ally McBeal, who she thought was cute. She did a good imitation of me, too, when she didn't like what I was saying.

"People just don't understand me," she'd whine, in my voice, balling her fist at the corner of her eye. Then in her own, harsh and spitting, "So why don't you go do them a favor?" I gave her the finger a lot in the beginning, but one day she did her Martha Stewart imitation, holding up a capsule she was supposed to take. Examining it closely, she said, "When I'm in a hurry, I have a special way of sticking this up my ass." When I laughed, she shouted, "She lives!" shaking her fists at heaven, then bowing down and pounding the carpet, "Thank you, Lord," and crossing herself like a Catholic. I had to laugh again. "Two in one day," she said, "you're going to have a heart attack, that is if I don't first."

Now I kissed her on the cheek.

"Take care, girl."

I set my suitcase behind the stone fountain and looked for a place to hide. I remembered the trees as being closer. I'd thought to hide behind one so I could see them park and watch them as they walked around, trying out the swing, maybe, looking up at each passing car.

Instead, it was me looking up when they drove into the parking lot and Mom pulled up to the fountain, where I was standing. How long did we stay frozen like that? Mom and Diana staring from the front seat and Molly peeking through the space between them.

Then things happened so fast, I can hardly separate them in my memory. Mom put the car into park. The engine died. All three doors opened, and I could feel myself turning, ready to run, but they were too fast. I was in their arms, and then my knees were buckling, "oh god, oh god," someone was saying—could it be my voice? Then Molly, "I love your hair like that." Mom just smiled and pressed her forehead against mine, then pulled me toward the car. And Diana, when I turned back, saying, "I'll get your bag."

That emotional maelstrom is still a beating at the back of my throat. I pull out a pad of paper and a pen from the drawer in the coffee table.

Dear Myself,

Everyone knows a piece of you, and yet no one knows the one piece.

Why don't you tell it? Take it out of the dark. Unpack it from the backseat of the car.

It's not true what Grandma said, that we all went to bed early that night.

You were busy sliding behind the driver's seat as he ran back to the house for his keys, his hand wrapped in a towel. Why did Mom give up so easily when he said he wanted to go alone? She should have seen that he was crying. All the way down the driveway that horrible sobbing and cursing. "I hate my life."

What had we done to make him so sad? You still had your pillow in your arms, because you were going to sleep alone in the tent that we had set up that day and surprise everyone in the morning. You buried you face in it and curled up as tight as you could behind him.

But you must have made a noise, because suddenly his hand was on your back. "Is that you, Cecily? What the—" and then the car stopped so loud and hard it hurt to move. The dome light had gone on, and when you looked over the edge of the back seat, what got your attention was the windshield, which looked blistered, like a window covered in frost. A line started just above his head and reached toward the passenger side, traveling slowly like a long skinny finger. When it reached the door and started creeping into the passenger window, you slammed your shoulder against the door and jumped out.

Daddy's door was stuck and something under the hood was ticking. You went to the passenger door. From outside, the creeping line looked sad. Keeping your eye on it, you opened the door and crawled in, still clutching your pillow. You tried to get him to wake up, but his eyes were closed and there was no room to get your hand in between his neck and the steering wheel. So you waited. His poor hurt hand was lying in the seat between you. You picked it up and rewrapped the bloodied towel around it.

There was a big bump when the car moved and started sliding, and it made him groan. His forehead was the only part you could reach, so you patted it, but your fingers came away bloody. You stole a glance at the creeping crack.

He sighed.

You pushed the pillow partway into his lap, rubbing your fingers on it, and bolted.

You had to tell! But what if you did this. You stopped in the middle of the road and looked back at the car where the line now reached the ground, a long split in the earth racing toward you. Mom's car was coming down the driveway, so you hid in the culvert and waited till you heard her car door slam. She was going after him. She felt bad letting him go alone.

Then she screamed, and you took off again for home, only you had to hide behind the big pine when Grandma came running down the drive.

Mom never asked why your pillow was in Daddy's lap.

But when would she have noticed?

It's not just the splinter finger pointing at you or the folding windshield. Tell her! Show her this letter. Not because it's the magic key that explains why you've been such a disappointment, but because it doesn't belong to you, not anymore.

My Silver Bowl

I saw right away why they needed me, what with Meredith a professor at the university and three little girls needing someone to look after them after school and such. I knew that her husband got killed in a car wreck less than a year ago because one of my friends works in her building, which is Environmental Sciences, and she explained the situation to me when I told her that I was going to pick up a new house to keep.

She has a nice face to look at, but you could tell she still suffered because she had a sad expression even when she smiled. When I handed her my resume, she spells out my last name and says is that Sigh-eed? At first I didn't get what she was talking about.

"No, it's SAID as in, that's what I said."

She laughed, and I added getting her to smile to my job description. I always wanted to have teeth like that, where you could run your finger smooth and easy along them, not the up and down of mine like one of those roads they had in the olden days, made of logs stuck side by side in the mud. At the first rain they'd be budging up against each other every time a wagon passed over.

That's what you call a simile, which is at the top of my vocabulary list in Introduction to Literature. I'm a junior now, after twelve years. William, which is my husband, says it's time to declare my major (which I already did, he just never remembers, it's called General Studies). He thinks it's high time I decided what work I'm going to do, because with a college degree you can do better than mopping floors and emptying trash cans and cleaning people's houses on the side.

I had Nutshell in my pocket, a sweet brown kitten that almost died of dehydration after she was found walking crazy outside my building and someone brought her to me. The little one, Molly, heard her mewing and came running. While Meredith and I talked, Nutshell poked her nose out and got snatched away. The girls begged their mother to let them have her, but she said no, that their grandmother is allergic.

I could see early on that Meredith let them get away with a lot. Except the oldest one named Diana who didn't do anything bad. She told the others to behave and not act like heathens, that was her word for them. Molly was like a little boy except for the long braid. Always in torn jeans and a t-shirt, running in from outside and letting the door slam. She'd holler, "Sorry," but never let it close easy. And Cecily was the moody one. I'd catch her looking at me out of the corner of her eye whenever we were in the same room for any length of time, like when she was sitting at the kitchen table coloring or watching TV while I was making dinner. Once I said, "What are you looking at?" and she just rolled her eyes.

One day Cecily was moping about how boring summer was, so I says, "I've got an ideal. Let's make a trifle." Molly was drawing one of her pictures of horses. She pauses a moment and says, "Don't you mean idea, Mary?" I tell her that's what I said, but she claims I said ideal and that's a different word. I started thinking about those two words and how I thought they were the same. I never paid attention till then. So at home I caught myself saying ideal but pinching off the L and feeling like the word wasn't finished. But that's what happens when you step into a house like that, where a six-year-old can tell you how to pronounce a word and then run over and stand between your legs, leaning her back against you so you can both look at her picture together, her holding one corner and you the other.

This was a house in mourning. Three girls on edge. Feelings hurt and getting mad, yelling or slamming doors, or in Diana's case, setting her mouth in a firm line and jutting her chin out. How many tears I dabbed with a Kleenex I couldn't begin to guess. I never saw their mother cry, but for the first year or so, she was always at wits end. When Cecily locked Molly in the trunk of the car one day and then got absorbed in afternoon reruns, she didn't notice that all of us were calling for Molly. Like she was in her own world. Then Meredith goes out to the car because she's going to the grandmother's place to look for her, which is only a ways down the road, and she hears Molly banging on the trunk hood. Luckily, it was October and not the dead of summer. She fell asleep and then woke up mad as a nest of hornets. Up she marches to the house, into the TV room, taps Cecily on the shoulder, and when she doesn't turn around, socks her right in the side of the face. That woke her up, and the next thing they're rolling on the floor and Meredith is pulling Cecily away and I've got Molly and I'm saying, "Shame on you girls," and Meredith goes, "What on earth were you thinking, Cecily?"

"Molly," she says, turning to her youngest and pulling her close, "use your words, not your fists." Molly says, "She's a self-ish little bish." It's not the first time I've heard her use that kind of language, but with the gap from missing front teeth, it comes out "bish," which brings a laugh up from my gut, which I have to pinch back. I look to Meredith to see what she will say. But she is in calm-down mode and just pulls both girls close and looks at them at eye level.

"Molly, there's no need to call names. The point is, Cecily, Molly could have been hurt and you need to look out for her better than that. Now both of you, go clean up. Cecily, you use my bathroom. You've got extra chores tonight."

And that's it for the moment, though there was a couple more shoves on down the hall that Meredith pretends not to notice. Molly sticks her tongue out and Cecily flips her the bird. That was the way those two were, something always sticking up or poking out, like a foot when the other walks past.

But they were loyal too. The only way you could get one to tell what the other was up to was if they were fighting. Close, in love and war. I think because they were born the same day three years apart, Cecily thought Molly was hers and when Molly got too independent it riled her. But no one could say a bad word about Molly without Cecily comes back with a snotty remark that shut you up good. I speak from experience.

One time after I was going there for a few months, I found Molly sticking an entire bag of baby carrots under her shirt and making for the door. This was soon after their grandmother got them each a horse, so I knew where she was headed. I said, "No you don't Miss Molly," and up snaps Cecily's head. I notice but don't pay her any heed and say to Molly, "You get back in here with them carrots 'for I tan your hide. I need those for the pot roast tonight."

"Mary Said, 'You know how my mother disapproves of violence.' If you can't set an example you'd best keep your mouth shut."

I turned around to give her a piece of my mind, and that's all Molly needed to scoot out the door. "I would appreciate if you'd show a little more respect," I tell her, and she's right back with, "R-E-S-P-E-C-T, tell you what it means to me," dancing with her fanny out and her finger stirring the air. I suppose it was funny but I was mad for a good two hours and wouldn't look at her or answer her, even when she took a phone call that was William. I waited till she set the phone down with a "suit yourself," before I picked it up and told my husband I had a good *ideal* to share with him later. (I think you could call that irony, which is when you say something that you don't mean so everyone knows you don't mean it, or when it refers back to something earlier and sheds a new, maybe funny or chin-rubbing light on it.)

That has been my life with this family for better than two years. I get off work at 11:00, go to whatever class I can schedule during the lunch hour, then head to their house till 5:00, except when Meredith goes to a conference, and then their grandmother stays there all the time and that gives me a few days off. It makes for a 12-hour day and then home to dinner that William fixes because he's not like most men. I always spend a couple of hours with whatever cats and dogs I'm taking care of till a home is found. I've never needed more than six hours sleep a night, and that's what I get, in bed by 9:00, up by 4:00, when I make Will's lunch and mine and share a cup of coffee before we go our separate ways.

For a couple of hours the house is quiet, and I can catch *Days of Our Lives* and *The Young and Restless* while I clean and get dinner started before the girls get home and things get lively (as in the above examples). Gradually they got to where they would come and hang out with me in the kitchen. Cecily especially likes to hear about my people. That's how she says it, "Tell me about your people when you were little." She likes to hear about the times I ran away and how I'd get the switch when I came back, and she likes to hear me talking in my mama's voice, "You like to scared me to death. How I gointer get everything done around heah ifn you leave for parts unknown?" She likes to hear about my seven brothers, the last two of which were my job to care for after Mama got sick. They get sad when they hear how her death was long and how she cried out for God to take her home. I didn't like to talk to them about death, but they were morbid. I prefer to tell them about Little Will's job as a roughneck working on an oil rig in Alaska. I tell them Will doesn't call too often and doesn't write at all, but I do know he can't get the smell of oil out of his skin even if he showers three times. Molly's mouth is round like a quarter. I push the tip of the iron into darts and fit the sleeve around the curved top of the board. Then it's time to set the table.

Sometimes when I first get there, after I deposit my coat in the kitchen, I like to go stand in the center of the house. It's a beautiful old open house, not like any house I ever lived in. With my back to the front door, I can look to my right and see the sun shining in through the windows of the big living room (also called TV room). Between the two big windows is a fireplace and beside it a big geode that Meredith says came from somewhere out west. It must weigh 300 pounds and is impossible to dust, what with all the pointy crystals, but it's pretty. I always look at it first. Then I look to my left and see the kitchen, with the big table and the breakfast bar separating the coloring room from the cooking part. Straight ahead is a hallway and stairs going up to the girls' rooms. If you go past the stairs and straight down the hallway you come to Meredith's room on the right and her study on the left, where she's got eight tables of rocks and minerals laid out in rows with neat little signs. Each one says what the rock is and where it came from. There's an order to them, but it's not color or size. I try to figure it out sometimes and think it's shape till something rears up in the middle of a row of flat pieces and there goes that theory. I do not dust in that room, but it's okay to vacuum.

Every day I do a different cleaning chore, though some more than once a week (like sweeping the kitchen). Dusting is a once-a-week job, fortunately, and one day while I was dusting her bed-side table, I accidentally pulled out the drawer and there it was, her personal diary. Curiosity got the better of me. Once I started reading I couldn't put it down. It wasn't that day but maybe the next when Diana came home early with cramps, and I realized how easy it would be to get caught. It turned out that Meredith was going to a caving conference that weekend, and on Friday after she left I checked to see if she'd taken it with her, and she didn't, so I took it home with me and made a copy and brought hers back and put it away. That way I could read it at home and no one need know. Her writing is little and neat, and she'd been writing in it almost every day since she found herself a widow.

I wait till William goes to bed to start reading. Poof Papa is the oldest, and he gets first lap choice. Little Will named him for being big daddy of a long line of champion mouse catchers. Skitter and Puppet make a place in the cave along my side, and Chewy the King of Lazy comes over and lies at my feet. In my Intro to Lit class, we filled out a little card that said what kind of reading we like to do. She read what I said out loud (anon). "I like to read so I forget where I am and who I am and become someone in the book for a little while." I decide to read just the first entry or two, but it turns out this is hard to do, as she doesn't start each day out with the date. I can only tell it's a new entry because she skips some space and usually the writing is a little different, like she was tired when she finished.

Today in class we read a short story by William Carlos Williams about a doctor who uses a wooden spoon to force open this sick girl's mouth. When Dr. P says that this was a sexual allusion, and that the wooden spoon was a metaphor for a man's thing, the class goes berserk. "You're reading too much into it," says one boy. "He's just trying to save her life, and if that's a violation (that was Dr. P's word) then it's sometimes necessary to use force when people are too stubborn to know what's good for them." So I said, "Then why does the doctor feel shame?" and Dr. P looked at me approvingly. So now I'm adding allusion and symbol to my list of terms. When you allude to something you're beating around the bush, not saying it exactly, but close enough so that if they're paying attention, your reader will know the words refer to something that was already done (in a totally different book). This is similar to symbol, because a symbol is also more than what it looks like. It takes on other meanings and becomes more powerful than it would be otherwise. Like the American flag. Or a rose. Or even a rock, maybe. Like, my cup runneth over.

I feel good about myself asking that question in class, because usually I'm real quiet, but that doctor gets me mad, and I can just see him straddling that little girl and thrusting that spoon (if you know what I'm alluding to) down her throat. Then before class is out she tells us that our final project, which is coming up in about three weeks, should be our own poem or short story, but no more than five pages. "Write about something you know," says Dr. P, but I'm tired of what I know and would like to try my hand at something I don't know. Maybe a story about an astronaut who gets stranded on the moon with only thirty days supply of food and air, which would allow me to say anything I want, because no one in this class has been to the moon. Or maybe tell a story from the point of view (which is not opinion but where you stand) of a fat, lazy cat. This entertains me all the afternoon as I'm cleaning. I could call him Malice of Foresight, which I always liked the sound of (and which could make this an allegory).

Today the girls have sniffles and just want to watch TV when they get home. I make some orange juice and chicken soup, which is what Meredith asked me to do, in a note she left for me: "The recipe you used last time would be great. See you a little early tonight. –M"

I have Miss Piggy with me because the shelter is full and they needed me to take care of her and her litter of four kittens. I get the girls to help me feed them, and I'm not surprised to see that it's Molly who stays with it, all afternoon, even though I can tell she's feeling bad. By the time I get home I'm feeling a little stretched myself, but I have some of the soup (which Meredith lets me bring home when I make a big pot of something). It is so good that William has seconds and then he goes to his armchair to watch a game and I go sit down at our first ever computer and start my story. The problem is that after I write for a long time and then read back over it, it sounds so stupid I hold down the delete button till it's all gone, which takes about five minutes. Meanwhile I watch Miss Piggy licking her babies. She looks up at me and opens her mouth to make little meow sounds that I can't even hear. While she's inside all the other animals have to stay out or the fur will fly. And that is not figurative language. Being excluded in this way makes them unhappy, so I always lock up Miss Piggy and her kittens in Little Will's room when I go to bed, and let the others back in.

The next day I'm too sick to go to work, and my supervisor says, "Get plenty of rest and drink lots of fluids," just like she's a doctor or something, but I appreciate her not getting on to me, which would be pretty ridiculous considering I haven't taken a sick day in three years. I call Meredith and say I'd better not come in, and she says, "Rest and drink lots of water." I take everyone's advice (plus Mama's hot toddy) and go to bed with the diary, which I read till I fall asleep, then wake up and read some more.

It makes me sad to think of Meredith, haunted by things that happened and didn't happen alike. I read the part about him dissolving when she saw him wavering in the distance. *When I lifted my eyes, I could see myself in the recliner looking around, and at the same time I could feel the hair rising on my neck. I quick shoved the diary where I always do, under a stack of coffee table books that we never look at anymore.*

Maybe I could write my story about a woman who gets amnesia and then can't tell whether what's going on in her head are echoes of the past or fantasies of what she'd like to happen. I wake up at 3:00 still in my chair with the alarm going off in the bedroom.

One week later my story is thirteen pages long. I notice that I am having trouble bringing it to a close. How does she get her memory back? Who is she really? These questions are not so easy to answer. I think I'll have a deus ex machina come along, but Dr. P seems not to have much respect for them, so I delete the big pick-up that's driving towards her. But something goes wrong and the whole story disappears. It's gone! As if it never happened, and since I didn't get around to making a back-up copy, I'm sunk, and this week a busy one. It's William's 50th birthday and his mother is coming over from Paducah and I'll be putting her up at the house, and that means trying to keep her from doing our laundry or reorganizing the bathroom cabinets and probably climbing up on the stool and falling and breaking a hip and ending up staying here for three months. I say screw it to this story because I'm beginning to see why Dr. P says we should write about something we know.

Cleaning floors, emptying trash, dusting, separating recycling from left-over Subway sandwiches and pizza crusts. All of the sudden I'm dividing the piece of paper in front of me into two columns. At the top of one, it says Meredith, and at the top of the other it says Mary. And here's how the words line up: successful…failure, beautiful…plain, nice legs…fat legs, nice teeth…bad teeth, educated…ignorant, all men want to sleep with…only one man will sleep with. A person that the past has overlooked and the future isn't going to smile on.

I turn the paper over and at the top write: Thoughts about My Short Story. Maybe I could make it about a housekeeper at WKU who discovers that someone is trying to poison the head of the English department. She finds a container of arsenic in the recycling and is muttering about how inconsiderate some people can be when she notices the skull and crossbones (which are a symbol) on the cover. She holds it by her fingertips, knowing the police will want to lift prints off of it, and then deposits it in a trashcan liner and drops it in her smock pocket.

My week from hell is over . . . I shouldn't say that. William was real sweet on his birthday and surprised too. Little Will called and talked to William because I was outside feeding the dogs, and William told me later he was coming home, that he has had enough. Mother Said was better than usual, helping me peel vegetables and measure and sift flour, and only once tried to clean up the laundry room. Fortunately, the box of detergent I just bought knocked over and made a big spill in the middle of the floor, and four cats darted away and then came back to investigate, which got her and the cats to sneezing, so I cleaned it up and she felt bad and said she'd stay away from that room. One room at a time, I almost said. (Which is mean.)

Finally, the night before my story is due, I decide to write a story about a housekeeper at Western, but leave out the part about the rat poison. I decide there will be a frame, which means a story that has another story inside it, and the inside story is her secret identity as a novelist, and the novel she's writing is about a woman whose husband has died and left her to pick up the pieces.

The denouement (day-knew-maw) comes when the housekeeper's husband really does get killed and she's going to end up living the life of her character. I don't know what you call that, but there's probably a name for it.

So I type like mad and save every five minutes and have everything done but the part inside the character's head, which I can't figure what to say about, then it hits me, that Meredith's diary might help me out. I need to find a passage that doesn't give up who wrote it, and here's what I pick out: *I need an explanation that will allow me to face the days ahead with something that will lighten this ton of rocks I carry in my heart. It aches and aches. It pulls my posture down in front and makes my back a shaft of barbed wire. What's inside is outside, what's out is in. The only way to put things back is to know why.*

Today I make a beautiful apple pie. It's fall and Diana and Molly and Cecily are all trying to take the peels off the apples in one piece. Diana is the best. Molly eats the peels that break off so she can say hers came off in one piece. Cecily gives up and asks to roll out the dough instead. By the time Meredith comes home, the smell of pie is everywhere. She sets down her book bag and before I get a look at her, she says, "Can we talk a moment, Mary? Girls, go watch TV for a few minutes."

"Sure," I say, wiping my hands on a towel and turning around. I can tell right away that something is wrong.

"Today I had lunch with Dr. P, and she was very complimentary about a story you turned in. She even read a little bit of it to me." She's got this look, but it's nothing like what I'm feeling, because my heart is up my throat and I'm having trouble breathing.

"Where did you get the idea?"

"Well, I don't know, I guess I had a lot of ideas and tried two or three different stories and each one kept getting lost or I couldn't figure out how to end and each one sort of had pieces of the other ones and it was the night before so I just wrote something." I'm babbling like a blooming idiot, which is what Mama used to say when she caught me lying.

"Have you read my journal, Mary?"

Three thoughts go through my head so fast it takes no time

at all. I can say no and how it must be a coincidence. I can act confused and ask if it was in a red binder or a blue one and throw her off that way. Or maybe I could get a coughing fit and have to leave the room, or maybe a heart attack and just die right now.

"Yes," I finally say, and my voice is so low she has to lean toward me.

"Why?" she cries out, her voice cracking and tears filling her eyes. "It was private!" She's gripping the back of her head. I'm frozen at the counter, my hands twisted in the dish towel. I have not seen her cry in all the time that I've been here, and now it's because of me.

"I'm sorry," I choke out, "I didn't mean any offense. I'll get my things."

Because I'm not going to make her have to say the words *You're fired.* She has left anyway, gone to her bedroom and closed the door. I stop in the TV room and take my last look at the girls. "Good-bye," I say. Diana waves her fingers without turning to see me, so my last image is of her hair pulled back in a ponytail and curled like a question mark. Cecily gives me a little look like she can tell something's going on and says, "Good-bye, Mary Said," all formal. "Molly?" I say, and she says, "I know, I know," then grabs the drawing she's been working on and brings it to me. "I want you to have this. My horses are getting much better, aren't they? It's for making us the apple pie and stuff." She pauses, then adds, "But if you think Little Will would like it, you can send it to him." Then I get a hug and she wiggles her finger for me to lean down, and I get a kiss. "See you tomorrow," she says. I leave then and cry all the way home, where I think I will never face another person except William.

It's been a month. I have three years of sick leave which I take. Maybe I'll take this year's vacation time too, and maybe I'll just crawl in a cave and die, because that's what I feel like I'm in: the darkest, loneliest cave you can imagine, and what's worse is I'm in the cave that's in me. William has stopped chewing me out and telling me to stop feeling sorry for myself and is now starting to look worried and giving me backrubs and patting me on the shoulder till I tell him to go take a hike. What's worse than William is not being able to escape *People's Court* and Judge Joseph Wapner in my head. It goes like this:

What's the big deal! I disguised my story so well Dr. P didn't know. If no one knows and no one is hurt, why does it matter? All this time, Meredith has been happy with me, and she had nothing but praises and hugs for me. I'm still the same, the same person. Why does she act like I'm someone else? Maybe I just needed to know what it's like to lose your husband because if William was to die, I'd be left alone, except for my animals. Maybe I did it without malice.

And then Judge Joseph says how stupid it was to put something private, even if you disguised it, into a story you were going to turn into a professor. So what if you didn't expect Dr. P to share it with her? You're a silly woman who has no business trying to get a degree. You can't even do your own work because it takes BRAINS to be educated.

William asks, "Does she know you made a copy of it?"

I give him a look and he puts his hands up and backs off.

When I go back to work, everyone is full of questions, but I know how nosy they are so I just say I was sick with a rare form of hypertension. I have to take another cleaning position because that's the only way I can afford to pay for food and shots for my babies. Finally, it turns to summer, and I stop looking back at that ugly winter. One day when we had just finished giving the dogs their yearly shots, I was gathering up the needles and William started horsing around. I threatened to jab him and pretty soon I had him on the run and we were laughing like a couple of fools, and then Little Will pulled in. When he stepped out of his truck, I ran to hug him and he saw me coming with the needles in my fist and jumped back in the car and made a show of locking the doors. We laughed, but I was crying.

"This here is Wolf. I liberated him from a dog fight," he says, after we hug and I point to the big dog standing at the door of the truck. He's a wolf-husky cross with long, coarse gray and brown fur. In the late afternoon, after Will has rested up with a nap, we all have a beer. Wolf and Poof eye each other, and Poof goes over and sniffs. I can see his whiskers curving forward. He must decide Wolf's okay, because he rubs his back against him and jiggles his tail in Wolf's face. Wolf looks at Will like he's sorry and won't do it again.

"They'da killed me if they caught me," Will says. "I was going to grab whatever dog I could, I was so pissed off. They were in a big hangar next to the shed where the actual fights was going on, and I wandered over there and stuck my head in, and this big dude grabs my arm and tells me to get out. It was the second day of this marathon fight and over his shoulder I could see a pen full of dogs from the night before, too wounded or dead to bother each other. I saw the whole thing like a photograph, cages lined up in groups and these big apes watching over them. I left and that's when I saw it . . ."

I cover my ears, but I hear anyway.

"I walked out and headed away, like I was leaving, then circled around, and off to one side I seen a pile of dead dogs. I thought I was gonna to be sick. Eyes torn out, legs ripped, guts spilling out, blood dried in a big frozen puddle. I step on something and then see it's a long black leg, probably from a part-wolf. I did get sick then. I seen men fighting, people starving to death, birds and seals coated with oil. I never want to see nothing like what I saw that night."

I have to get up and go to the bathroom. How can people be that way? For money! I press toilet paper into my eyes. Will calls out, "Sorry, Mom, I won't say anymore." I splash my face. Of all the people in the world, my husband and my son know how I get. I go back because I want to hear how he found Wolf.

"I went back to the fight barn and drank some beer and waited till the first fight was getting started. I saw more Huskies, Pits, some Dobermans, I don't know what all else. Just a stinking mess of dogs and men who'd sooner cut your throat as look at you. I headed back outside. I don't know why I didn't see him when I went by before. Maybe he was a special attraction. I didn't look to see if anyone was watching, just unhooked the chain and walked like he was mine back to the truck. Drove like hell outta there. I figured you'd be able to bring him back, if anyone could."

"I can't have him fighting with the others."

"He's more scared than anything. I think he's confused."

Will says he's thinking about seeing what work there is in welding, which he's real good at, and maybe find a place in the country to buy. He says he saved most of what he made and has a good down payment. It's good to hear him wanting to live here in Kentucky. "Most boring place on earth."

Wolf is skittish, but I work with him every day after work and on weekends, even let him sleep by my side of the bed, so he gets attached to me. Then I take him through the little training ring I've set up. I'm teaching him to jump and crawl in addition to the usual commands that any cared for dog knows. The more tricks a dog learns, the happier they are. Dogs' number one goal in life is to please people (unless they're starved, beaten, or neglected). Maybe Wolf has some dog in him. If he goes after one of the other dogs, I make him go to his doghouse. He puts his head between his paws and all he has to stare at is a brown field and row of trees. But where some dogs have to be kept in the fenced yard, Wolf doesn't run. Unlike Chewy the Sly One, he doesn't sneak to the front and then act as if everything is normal. One time I forgot him and it wasn't till I was getting ready for bed that I looked out and saw him watching me in the lighted window. He stays close, too close half the time, tripping me and knocking against me every other step. I realize I'm crazy about that dog, his coarse fur, his one blue eye that shades over into gray at night, his curly tail and his straight up pointing ears, each one a fist full.

Over time, we settle into our usual pattern of life. Up before dawn, early to bed, lots of animals, endless work. Will comes by every couple of weeks, but I can call him any time and he'll come by and give us a hand. I work for three or four people, sometimes six months, sometimes a year, and finally find a situation that looks like it will last. Same set-up as I had with Meredith and the girls, only this time it's boys and they live in town.

One spring day I build a series of tunnels with bales of hay, so I can teach Wolf to crawl through them, something he used to know how to do but has forgotten, as I've been too busy to keep up with his lessons. A car pulls up in the driveway and some girl I've never seen before waves at me and then walks over.

"You don't recognize me, do you, Mary Said."

It's Diana, I see, though her hair is short now. I tell her I would never forget her face, even after four years, or is it five, and she hands me an envelope and says it's an invitation to her graduation party.

"That's an amazing looking dog you've got there."

"His name's Wolf, my son brought him back with him from Alaska."

"Is he a wolf?"

"Part . . . trouble is, I don't know which part," I say, a little joke I've developed.

By now Wolf knows we're talking about him so he trots over to get his ears rubbed. I tell Diana to tell him to roll over and slip her a dog treat to give him.

"You always have the neatest pets. I remember the kitten you had in your pocket the first day you started working for us. . . . So will you come?"

I'm looking down at the card and getting ready to answer, when she says, "You know we missed you a lot after you left. Cecily and Molly want you to come too." She pauses a moment, then says, "And Mom, too, of course."

I've got three days to think about it and it seems like that's all I do, which gets on my nerves, especially when it's midnight and I have to get up in three hours.

When I pull into the driveway, my hands are shaking, but I tuck my packages into my big bag and step out of the car. There's young people everywhere but they just look through me as I head into the house. As soon as I step into the kitchen, I feel faint. I'm trying not to look too hard and hoping I see them before they see me. But it doesn't happen that way. Molly sees me and I just can't help crying when she walks over to me, so tall and sure, and gives me a hug. Then she tucks her arm under mine and leads me over to Cecily, who is hanging around a table they've got set up at the foot of the stairs for champagne. "May I see your ID?" she says. Her face is flushed, and she sways when she hands me a glass. I see that it's Cecily who is the real beauty of the three. Why didn't I ever notice that before?

My bag has slipped off my shoulder and the champagne jumps a little out of the glass. "I guess I'd better drink this before it spills," I say, and Cecily fills the glass again.

"Bottoms up!" she says, and when I say, "My, Cecily, you're so grown up," I can see that she is proud of herself.

"Mom!" Molly calls out and I look up at Meredith coming toward us, her brown hair a cloud around her face. I go to set my glass down and my bag falls off my shoulder again and makes the champagne jump. There's an awkward moment while I'm rubbing the champagne off my fingers.

"Hello, Mary, I'm glad you could come." She sounds like she means it and her smile is enough to steady me. Then someone else pulls her away and I catch my breath. I give Diana my gift. It's only $20, but I tucked it into some WKU running pants, and tell her I hope that's where she's going to college next year.

I sit with Cecily awhile and see the kitchen is pretty much as I left it. Molly takes me out to the barn to see Babe, who is in the stall next to Cecily's horse Iago.

"She's a beautiful horse," I tell Molly. "And fast too?"

"Like the wind," she says.

"Well, that's plenty fast."

"Yep, especially on a windy day."

We both laugh and then I decide it's time to head back, so she walks me in and I go to use the bathroom. But when I pass the study I stop. Her rocks are in cases along the walls now, fancy ones that pull out and are lit up by hidden track lights.

"It's different, isn't it," she says, to my left, as I turn from the doorway. "I got a grant to do some research."

"I'm glad for you."

"And I'm glad for you!" she says, taking my hand to shake it. "Congratulations on the award. I never knew you were such a rescuer of animals!"

She's referring to the university award I just got for service, because of the work I've done over the years with the Humane Society and the rescue leagues for different breeds. I can feel myself blushing, and then, as if no time has passed, I'm blustering again.

"You know, I used to make lists comparing me to you and I always came out looking worse. You know, like you're educated and I'm not, and you're beautiful and I'm homely as a mud fence."

She shakes her head. "No. No. No. You are not plain and I am certainly not beautiful. I remember the day you came to interview. I had already interviewed two women who would have been good, and then you came, and I could tell you were the right one. I told my mom, 'She has a good and gentle face,' and then you won the girls over."

She takes my arm and we start to walk out. Then she stops and says, "Now you have a new item for your list." She holds her hand up and writes in the air, "Saver of lives over here under this column and saver of rocks over here."

That night as I'm falling asleep, I think about something my history professor Dr. Cabott said during the last course I took before I graduated: "For me, the word discover is never innocent." My hand is writing in the air, in cursive, like a grade school teacher showing the class how to make the letters: e-n-v-y. I hadn't realized how it had took hold of me, how I was going through the motions of my life while my thoughts were caught up in someone else's life that I wanted for myself. Even when I told those childhood stories, it was to let the girls see another world, one they thought was mine.

I don't think I looked in a mirror for two years. I dreamed of drowning. I could see the shore come close, something beautiful and known, and then before my feet could touch the sand, my weight would pull the waves around me. My award came as a surprise. It's a silver bowl, which I have set between my pillow and William's. In it, a teacup poodle named Big'nuff is breathing heavily through her tiny nose. She has asthma, so if she has a fit in the middle of the night, I need to be where I can hear. Sometimes all she needs is reassurance. Last night when William turned off the light, I told him I was hopeful she would make it through the night. Tonight will be no different.

Early Blur

Funny how things come out when you're with someone you hardly know, like Will, or don't see very often, like Patrick. Patrick likes to talk an idea into the hereafter, so I don't have to do much but listen. Truth is, I grew up around intellectuals, so I knew who said what his T-shirt said yesterday, that the unexamined life is not worth living. On the hike in, Will said he thought maybe the only life not worth living was the one that isn't your own. Patrick said exactly.

For our first hunt, Patrick went off on his own, and I let Will follow with me. "I appreciate the invitation," he said, looking up into the treetops. "My dad would love it out here." His old man's a plumber who subcontracts for me, but I hadn't seen his son in a long time, due to him living in Alaska. I forgot he existed until I ran into him at Wal-Mart, sighting down a Ruger Pellet Rifle. "You go hunting any time recent?" he asks. Pity got to me or maybe something appealing about him, and now we've got an overnight trip to the rock house to find out.

His head was cocked back so he could see to the treetops, so I said, "Oaks have a lifespan of 800 years, though you won't find any half that old anymore. There's a white oak over 300 years old at Lincoln's old home near Hodgenville. The best white oak comes from trees over a hundred years old. The white oak acorn is the least bitter of the oak family, and squirrels love it."

He appreciated this information so much that he pointed his Ruger into the branches. At the same time, I took aim at a big guy in a neighboring tree. It's a heavy mast this fall and squirrels are fat and lazy. In the upper branches, he kind of drifts down, and then speeds up till he lands with a bounce of leaves. When we got back with my three, he announced, "You shoulda seen Ned get these, damn! Each with a shot to the head. Pop. Pop. Wish I could do that."

We pulled out the hamburger and Will invented the squirrger, which was a layer of roasted squirrel meat on top of a hamburger. We drank some beers.

"Want to hear a squirrel joke?" Will asks. We both say no. "Why do squirrels swim on their backs?" No answer. "To keep their nuts dry." Patrick lets out a little laugh. I say, "That one's older'n you are, boy."

"It ripens with age," he says, then looks at Patrick. "You married?" Patrick nods, "You?"

"Nah. I was married once for a brief while in Alaska, native style."

"How was it up there at the top of the world? Always wanted to see for myself."

"I worked on the rigs on the North Slope as a roustabout. In Barrow and Deadhorse, it's below freezing—I mean *way* below freezing—about ten months of the year. Other than that, it ain't bad. All winter there's a glow across the polar desert. I never did get tired of watching the Northern Lights. You can't imagine the kind of nature they got up there. I thought I was going to live there the rest of my life."

"What's the population up there?"

"Same question my mechanic asked. There's about 7,000 people living in Barrow. They got a community college, a wildlife sanctuary with millions of birds living there. So, besides the cold and the 24-hour dusk and the arctic birds and the wolves and the caribou and grizzlies and most of the people are Inupiat Eskimo, it's like anywhere else.

"Sun rises in May and sets in August. It's a long-ass day. So what's your wife do?"

He opens another beer. I get busy with a fire poker, knocking something off my boot.

"She used to teach high school, but she's taking a leave. Breast cancer."

"Damn. My mom had that, but they stopped it before they had to cut. They cut her?"

Patrick doesn't answer for a time and I can feel Will looking back and forth between us.

"She had both removed in March."

"So, will she keep teaching?"

"I guess she's going to get up in the morning and make break-fast for us or sit down and read the paper while I make waffles. Then she's going to spend the day weeding the garden or reading a book or writing in a journal she keeps or running errands or canning tomatoes. And come January she's supposed to go back to teaching. She won't wear the prostheses."

Patrick has a way of saying what's on his mind, so it leaves a picture you can't shake.

"Why not?"

"She doesn't like the way they feel. They ride up under her armpits, move around."

There's a pause while me and Will try not to look at what he just put before us.

"That must be hard. I mean rough. I mean, never mind." There was silence for a minute. Then, "Talking about personal shit is like walking across where a war was and you got to steer away from places where you'll get blowed up."

He looks up from where he's been staring into the fire but Patrick's right there with him. "Sometimes talking is the only way out of a place, like your voice is a map."

"Yeah, like that."

This strikes me as a good place to get on a different road, so I put on my turn signal. "On our way in you mentioned being on the wrong side of a shotgun a time or two."

"It's really only the one time I was deaf for twenty-four hours. I was dating Kate, and her brother had a problem with white people and caught up with me one night. He stood in the middle of the road with his shotgun pointed at my head. I stopped my truck and got out. We were already talking about getting married, so I had to face this asshole now or he'd plague me forever. He tried to scare me by talking Inupiat, but I just kept saying, we're getting married, ain't nothing you can do to stop it. He finally shoved the barrel into my face and I grabbed it and pointed it away and it went off as I was letting go. We wrestled around in the dirt till I wasn't so mad anymore and were friends after that.

"Kate's short for Katauyak. Her mother named her for a rainbow that appeared the day she was born. It's so far north that a rainbow can be a full circle. I guess she was the best thing that ever happened to me. So it was an evil day when . . ."

Will's voice had changed, like talking wasn't a map anymore but the shaky ground itself. He stared at the fire and then pushed at a log so sparks flew up.

"Do you care to say what happened?" Patrick finally asked.

He crushed the beer can and tossed it into the fire. Sparks lit the way into the sky and then went out.

"Kate was responsible for closing up, so the night she disappeared, she had $3,000 from the restaurant and bar tucked into her sled. She was a hard mix of traditional and modern, refused to own a car, used a team of six dogs to get around. But she was working on a degree, taking courses through the university at Juneau, online. A computer geek with a team of huskies.

"Her team showed up at our place. You'd think they mighta led us back to where it happened, but when we tried to get them to, all they did was stand in the middle of the road looking stupid. It was early winter, temperatures dropping. We looked for two weeks. I personally covered a 50-mile area.

"All winter I studied faces, trying to see something like a guilty conscience. It wasn't until April that someone saw an arm poking out of the snow. Not near town but all the way in an oil field a couple hundred miles away. It was the biggest tundra spill of the year, corroded pipes. That's a problem, pipes aging, and it's only going to get worse. Water runs through the lines and leaks between insulation and pipe walls, then eats at the metal. Actually, it wasn't so much oil as produced water—salt water and oil mixed. They use salt water to increase the pressure and improve the oil flow. Salt water's just as bad for the tundra as oil. Kills all the plants. That's what happened. A big meltdown of snow."

Darkness was pushing in, and the night sounds seemed to have stopped, just an occasional crackling as a twig broke behind us, and Will's story, hitting the air.

"She had a bullet in the back of her head and was clutching a necklace I gave her, silver chain with a whale hanging off it."

He cleared his throat.

"I took it off her and put it on me. It was too small, so I put it on another chain and kind of wrapped her chain around it. Wearing what she last had ahold of kinda worked into my mind. At first, I thought she was holding that necklace because she was thinking of me the moment she died, then I started to think about how we bought it from an opportunist up there—ain't no corner of this planet free of 'em. He was in town that week with a bunch of jewelry on trays, and I bought it for her the day before she disappeared. So, maybe she was pointing to who done it.

"I tracked him down. Just need to talk to the right people. He had a shack in Nuiqsut, on a gravel road, which is all there is up there. He was drunk when Kate's brother and me paid him a visit. Weird place. Had all these animal skulls hanging from the ceiling. You couldn't walk through it without banging into them. The deposit bag was under his mattress, $2000 of it left. I pulled my brother-in-law off him but not before a few ribs got broke. We turned him and the money into the police. Turns out after he killed her, he packed her in a crate and told a pilot it was equipment and flew back home and buried her where he thought no one would link her to the disappearance in Barrow, if she was even found. If you go any distance up there, except for truckers taking Haul Road into Deadhorse, you travel by air.

"I left before the next winter set in. On my way out, I stole a miserable wolf-husky mix used for dog fighting. That was for Katauyak."

The embers were pale orange and dark gray.

"We've got an early rising tomorrow, boys."

Patrick climbed into his bag by the fire, but Will moved his to the edge of the overhang. I know what he saw if he looked up. There's a circle of stars, and a breeze picks up the branches and lays them against the night, so the stars at the edge of the circle of night come and go.

The darkness of 5:00 in the morning is a different dark from the one we went to sleep in, though you can't measure it. The beam of the flashlight points to the back of the rock house, and in that tunnel of light, I get the fire going again and start the coffee. There's no coffee like what's made on a campfire, especially here in the rock house, where neither heat nor rain can get you. There's better'n a hundred rock houses like this one in Kentucky, big mouths at the base of cliffs. This one's middling in size. We built the picnic table, the fire pit, and stashed firewood over the years. The ceiling drops in the back, but there's a place where you can go further, if you crawl. My sister says it's a dead cave, which means there's nothing beyond the back walls, but the way Kentucky is, you can find an entrance to just about anywhere.

Patrick joins me at the fire. Will's snoring.

"Tough break about Will's wife," he says.

"Yeah. You never know, do you?"

We watch the shaggy pieces of hickory catch. The coffee begins to percolate.

"So, is Connie good, then?" I look in his direction.

"Getting there. Tonight's the first night I've been away." He pushes his thumbs into his eyes and laughs. "You know, we used to kid about her best feature, from this Holly Hunter line, but since her operation, all her features seem best—hands pushing in the dirt around a flower, her chin, her neck turned just so, the backs of her knees, even her elbow, where it showed through the sleeve of an old flannel shirt. I could linger on that hole in her shirt."

I hold my breath, uneasy.

"She used to say, it's not like it's my eyes or my ears. It wasn't as bad as this or that. At least the cancer was gone, the worst was over. But she missed the missing part. While I was appreciating new features, like I said, she was scratching the air. It's like an echo, she says she can feel them but they're far away."

He's stopped talking and looks over at Will, still snoring. I just clear my throat.

"Sometimes the only good to come out of a bad thing is knowing how much you can bear, and you didn't really want to know that anyway."

He laughs and this time it sounds like a laugh. "Shit, Ned, I didn't mean to go on. Something about being away from everything. How do you want to handle splitting up today?"

"Well, it's whatever you two want to do. I thought I'd head to the valley."

Patrick washes down a ham sandwich, then grabs the .22 I always loan him.

"I'll head back the way we came, leave these two ridges for Will."

Hickory is stronger than steel, and a cord has the same thermal units as a ton of coal. Green hickory cannot be beat for smoking meats. Three hundred years ago, the forests of Kentucky were some of the best in the country. This valley still has scores of shagbark hickory trees near two hundred feet tall, and same with oaks. There's sugar maple, sweet gum, tulips, mulberry. You don't know about them unless I invited you or maybe fly over. I grew up out here, hunting with my granddad and camping in the rock house half the summer. It's a good deer valley, what with the stream cutting through, and you can forget there's another world out there. That's why I don't bring many people out here, and when I do, I send them in the other direction.

Will thinks I don't know he's following me, but he's so used to clumping around with a welding helmet on his head, he's about as subtle as a backhoe. I step behind a cluster of blackberry bushes and wait. Pretty soon Elmer Fudd comes along with a gun over his shoulder. A couple of squirrels set up an alarm and he decides to take a look. Gets under a big oak and turns his cap around. He takes aim and fires, and a squirrel lands with a spray of leaves about twenty feet away. He's probably thinking there's more where that came from, maybe they're too full to move, so he aims back up to the tree. I slip away, silent as a deer fart.

I hear him blamming away for another twenty minutes before it's quiet again and the freed-up sounds of the forest slip out of the shadows. Squirrel, insect, a falling nut, the wind lifting the leaves and sending them in a blizzard back to the ground. Patrick's on the other side of the holler by now.

This here hollow oak is where I've caught a dozen squirrels with my old dog Rusty. The first time one of them jumped into this hole, I grabbed a five-foot piece of bramble and twirled it around till it caught the squirrel's tail and I could drag him out. He tried to dart away and when I yanked him back again, he tried to bite my head off. I dispatched him. Rusty said something to him about just trying that again, or maybe it was how grateful he should be that it wasn't Rusty's teeth that separated him from this world.

The hole is widening, growing taller, and up about ten feet or so, light's coming through.

This is the sort of valley where you can stand almost anywhere, throw your head back, and track the long planes of tree trunks rising to a distant blue. You can lose your balance if you don't plant your feet wide. If you're like me, it's not difficult to imagine living down here. Maybe taking up a craft, maybe building chairs from scratch the way that fellow does up in Berea that I read about in *Fine Woodworking.*

"Pull up this here chair that took 2,000 hours to make." You wouldn't say it unless you meant it.

You'd come out once in a while for groceries. Plant a garden. There's already half an old apple orchard, put in by my granddad when I was a kid. I've been dreaming this since I started my own business. The first year when there was anything left after bills, I started investing the profits. After about twenty years it adds up. It was hazy at first, but at the back of my mind I knew what I was saving for. Don't you want to travel, my sister used to ask. Go someplace you've never been. Get a specially bound Triple-A Trip-tik.

Sometimes, driving down the road toward home, I don't know where I am. Is Natcher Parkway up ahead or behind me? Is this my driveway? Along the stream is the best place to build, where you could sit on your front porch and watch the mist rise in the morning and the sun cut through the leaves. In winter, snow will collect along the banks in the shadows and form fist-sized caves of air above the chilling water. I'd want to do something with this rock table. You can sit on it and empty your head of all that clutter. It's a thinking rock.

I'll get back to you, something you say when you don't mean it. It comes out of my mouth without me knowing it, then lingers. Just a little more pollution. *I'll get back to you.* My sister calls it the disappearing factor. She thinks it's depression, more than natural inclination. You're always trying to slip away, she says.

I should have been born a couple hundred years ago. One of those crusty fellows you stumble across when you get lost and then can't find the place again. She thinks it's because my wife

Lilly left us. It's true that kind of sucked the air out of me, especially after that foolishness, following her to Ohio to try to win her back. Sonny was miserable, calls it the year from hell. Only good thing was we made friends with Patrick and his daughter. But I'm long over that.

Why does wanting to be alone have to mean something else?

Two deer come to the stream a hundred feet away. They don't see me, and I don't move. They drink then lift their heads and look around, but they're not concerned. One of them is young, about to face his first winter. The other is getting on in age, white around the nose.

Then they're off, startled by something. They dash by, still not seeing me.

It's a mid-life crisis, my sister said this summer when I told her I couldn't stand going to work anymore. You'll get over it. Don't flake out on us. She's not usually high-handed, but she never got over being older, and when I'm feeling puny it really kicks in.

Besides, maybe there is no getting over it. Maybe what I need is to get into it, not over it. Investment magazines like to print stories about how successful couples maximize their earnings. Smug, full of themselves, in their luxury homes, they say things like "It's important" and "It's not easy." Every once in a while, I stumble across an article, not in the investment magazines, about someone who's given up all that. They may still look puffed up, but they've got blue skies or the ocean or some other glimpse of nature behind them. They'd have nothing to say to the other couples, except it's important and it's not easy.

I look up into the black walnut, and separate from the leaves that float on the edges, I can see two clumps of mistletoe. The mistletoe gets its water and minerals from the tree. It doesn't kill the tree, at least not for a long time, just borrows from it . . . unlike kudzu, foot-a-night, my granddad called it, which strangles everything in sight. I used to dream of kudzu, or something like it.

When you get down to it, what would you really miss? After some initial longing, everything that seems so important would just slip away. Biggest shock for most people is when they find out they're replaceable. I haven't done anything that someone else couldn't have done just as well, except maybe raising Sonny, and he can take care of himself now. Collins Construction will provide shelter under any name. Only thing that no one can do for you is decide what's an acceptable amount of strangulation.

I hear them before I see the swans flying overhead. Trees are so thick, I glimpse only the right leg of the V. Put them on water and they're self-interested honkers, but when they fly, their wings beat together like it's one massive body sailing over. I can't remember ever seeing swans flying over Kentucky. Geese, never swans. Migrating birds don't change their route for no reason. They'll even look for a spot in sludge if it's where they've always landed. Still, it catches in my throat when they pass over, them mapping a new route south.

This walnut's not as big a tree as some, but it's hardy. Along its base, you can see where the tree has levered the rock table to the side, as if to say, there's room for us both here, if you don't care to move over just a little. I have to jump in order to reach the lowest limb and pull myself up. The limbs are spaced so it's easy as climbing stairs to the top. The stink of walnut surrounds me like someone unaware they're thinking out loud. Two-thirds up the trunk some initials with blistered edges are carved into the trunk: JC loves LC. My grandparents. I wonder if they came down to this spot back when they first got the property.

Pretty soon I can't see much beyond the tired browning leaves. The best I can do is look down into the clearing by the stream and imagine where the roofline would go. There'd need to be some trees cleared, but only enough to allow the sun to hit the shingles. It should be an easy slope, something you can lie down on without sliding off. I lower myself to a branch and balance there, so my arms dangle. My face fits into a V where the branch splits. One part goes this way along my right cheek, and the other reaches out to my left. At the ends of the branches the same leaves and walnuts, swaying under my weight.

Well, it's settled then.

On the way back I keep my eye open for ways to get materials back here. That will be a challenge, since you can't get a road back here without carving up the hills. I've got a buddy who has a helicopter, flies for the hospitals when they need to get someone to Louisville or Nashville in a hurry. I can hear him when I ask him to lower a few tons of lumber for me. Are you out of your mind? Then, it'll cost you, as he starts to get behind the idea. He once lifted a horse and its rider off an island in the middle of the Ohio when it was flooding. Horse almost had a heart attack getting ready to be lifted but went limp as a rag once he was in the air. No sense in struggling when nothing's making sense. Reminds me of the T-shirt Sonny used to wear, with a picture of that South Park towel who's always stoned, saying, "I don't know what's going on."

Maybe it's too much, living off the land. Maybe there's something halfway between breathing and strangling. But, a joint just a little out of square in one corner means a two-inch gap under the front door.

By the time I get back to the rock house, Will and Patrick have already packed. They're sitting on the picnic table. I can see six squirrels, gutted and skinned, laid out to look impressive. Will's pretty much on top of the world, especially when he sees I don't have anything.

It's easier hiking back, without the beer. Patrick is quiet, Will's singing out of tune, and every so often he throws out a question, which gets a half-hearted answer.

We were quiet in the cab as we headed back to my place, until Will said, "I ain't had this much fun since I can't remember. I thought it was going to be another boring ass weekend in Bowling Green, but it wasn't nothing like it. Those squirrels were practically flying. So how come you didn't get nothing, Patrick?"

"I did."

He waited, but when Patrick didn't say anymore, Will nudged him. "Come again?"

Patrick sighed. "I wasn't going to say anything, but …

"You ever hear of something called early blur? I was reading about it the other day. It's when you go into the woods and whatever it is you're hunting, that's what you see. It may be a turkey wattle is really a red bandana, or you think you see a rabbit's tail but it's really a pussy willow. Or someone's face and brown hat look like the back side of a deer."

I said, "I never heard it called that, but it for sure happens—probably more with big game. Not much in the upper branches to make you see what isn't there."

"Well, I got up to the ridge before they started moving, and got ready to wait, blending into a tree trunk. You could look up and see them crossing each other like cars on highways.

"Something out of the corner of my eye caught my attention. It was a gigantic squirrel, climbing down the tree to my left. Andre the Giant of the squirrel world.

"It made a big noise coming down, and by the time it landed, I knew it wasn't a squirrel at all, but a raccoon. One of its eyes was gone, and the other dangled from its socket. I found a stick to dig a hole with, but that was taking too long, so I picked it up by the tail and started back along the ridge. I couldn't see just leaving it. Every step I could hear the cartilage in the tail crackle. I kept thinking it would be dragging on the ground by the time I figured out what to do with it. Then I saw this huge sycamore. About a foot above eye level was a hole. Three big mushrooms at the opening, like sentinels. I dragged over a branch and stood on it. I managed to shove everything in except for the tail."

During the silence that followed, Will muttered, "Weird."

"Stranger things have happened," I said. "My granddad used to tell about the time he went hunting and came upon two bears. Turned out they'd gotten separated from a circus that was traveling around the state. My granddad helped track them down."

"Good thing he didn't mistake them for a squirrel," Will said. "Damn, Patrick, why didn't you keep the tail, so you could make a coonskin hat out of it?"

"That raccoon made me kind of ill."

"Well, you couldn't help it. 5:00, 6:00, it's another world out there. The first time I saw the northern lights, I thought it was a port of entry for angels returning to heaven. You go to a new place, get up a little earlier, you see things for the first time. That raccoon mighta been ill and dying. Could be you done it a favor. I wouldn't feel bad if I was you."

"That striped tail like someone's hair brushing the scalp of the fungus—I'm going to see that for a long time."

Will sighed. We had pulled into my driveway.

"One thing I know, I'd rather see the northern lights, than blow the head off a raccoon."

Will sighed again. "No, shit."

I couldn't help the sinking feeling I got stepping out of the cab and looking at my two-story colonial. We all shook hands and said we'd see each other later. Will took off. Patrick came in to use the bathroom, but I could see he was anxious to head home.

I was just as glad to see them go, though I had the damnedest time figuring out what to do. I went to my office and looked at paperwork for about ten minutes, checked the kitchen and noticed chopped onions stuck to the burners of the stove, took a shower and changed my clothes, then ended up in the living room, where I stood at the picture window overlooking Bowling Green. The Wal-Mart Supercenter lies two miles away and beyond that, the yellow arches look like surprised eyebrows. A little to the left is the high-rise dorm of Western Kentucky University and beyond that at the top of the hill, the oldest building on campus looks east. The phone rings and eventually the answering machine picks up. The grandfather clock that my mother gave me ticks a hollow beat. My ears pick up the pulse of my heart. Night will come, then sleep, then morning. This assurance goes with me as I retrieve my rifles from the back of the truck and carry them to the basement for cleaning.

Abandoned Quarry

I

Patrick's hands still held the book, though he had dozed off minutes before gravity pulled it from the arm of his reading chair and closed it with a thud in his lap. *The wave is itself. The wave is every other wave.* Later, his daughter's cat Veronica, feeling her way around the book, aroused him enough to make his way to his bed, turning out the light on his way. *Your suffering is your own and every person's.*

Another Friday night had slipped into Saturday, and when Patrick awoke, it was well after 9:00. In the kitchen he pulled out the makings for bacon, eggs, and grits. As the skillet heated, he lined the bacon in neat rows on the microwave plate, covered it with a paper towel, and called out, "Phyllis, breakfast!"

Hearing no response, he headed up the stairs to her bedroom.

A rainbow of saliva emerged from her open mouth and shimmered in the morning light. He watched Veronica watching it, her eyes round, her paw ready to—what? Phyllis would know. She had explanations, even for Veronica's smallest movements. If she rolled over, Phyllis would say, "She's tired of that position," and if the cat stared at nothing, "She's considering the bits of dust in the sunlight."

"Wake up, Sleepy Head. Can't you smell that bacon?" She opened her eyes when the cat's paw tickled her lips.

"Veronica," she sighed, then noticed Patrick. "Hi, Dad. What do you want?"

"It's more like what do *you* want? You want to sleep your weekend away?"

She threw off the covers and slid into her slippers, just like his, made for boys out of a sensible corduroy brown. She had insisted,

47

turning her nose up at the girlish ones he'd tried to show her. "No, no," she'd said, "I like to rub my fingertips against these ridges until they're all tingly. Those just make me want to blow my nose. Here, you try."

Two weeks ago, he'd overheard her talking to her best friend Laura. "Kelly told me my boobs are starting to flop when I walk down the hall," and, "Yeah, it means you're easy." He was reading in the study while she sat curled up with her phone in the living room. A pause, a giggle, "No way!" then a long account that brought him to his feet and then to the doorway where she would have seen him had she turned his way.

"They are *so* creepy. And what's worse is they only live a couple miles from me. Kevin and Vince are bad enough—but Doober, ugh! Have you ever sat behind him? Blackhead spillage. . . . So anyway, I'm walking down the hall yesterday, and one of them goes, 'Nice tits,' but he says it kind of hissing so I'm thinking maybe I'm hearing things . . . yeah, like 'pie slits.' 'Shy fits?'" More laughter. "'Nice pits!' that's the best one yet."

Patrick backed away from the doorway to his chair, where he stood for several moments, then went to the wall of books, to one shelf in particular, where he had a small collection of books on parenting. He picked out *Teen Years* and tried to recognize either himself or Phyllis in the descriptions of raging hormones, the need for affirmation, and the promise that "it's their job to push the boundaries and your job to keep them firm." He imagined himself drawing a line in the sand and Phyllis nudging it, trying to push him back, closer to some dangerous edge.

And then, last Saturday, as they headed into town for groceries, Phyllis blurted out, "I need some female things, you know."

He'd hesitated, about to comment on the progress of their neighbor's cornfields.

"You don't need to make faces. All I need is some underwear. . . . Okay, so I want a booby-holder." She was drawing a cat's face, using small, quick strokes, and had just finished shading the eyes except for the triangle of reflected light. She held it at arm's length. "So will you go with me and ask for it?"

"No, Phyl, I don't think I'll do that."

"They'll be grown-ups there. You'll know how to relate on their level. Those old ladies will want to feel me up or something."

In the end he went in and bought three of them, using the chest measurement she'd given him and selecting the plainest white with no padding. "I want it to look like a sports bra," she had instructed him. She waited in the car and when he returned, he could tell she'd been chewing on her lip again, pulling thin strips of skin with her teeth. He tossed the bag to her. "Wait till we get home before you try them on."

"Duh."

He glanced at her bent head as she looked through the bag, her fingers working the plastic bag, until she'd poked a hole in it and was fingering the fabric inside.

"I wonder what Mom would have gotten for me."

That was her way, to bring her in at odd moments, her mother, who had said to him, "I feel so penned in. You're so boring. All you want to do is stay home. It's like you're fifty instead of thirty." And she'd hated the small town, longed for Chicago, leaving after their biggest fight and after dropping Phyllis off at school.

"You'd rather hang out with ideas. And you don't really like me, just the idea of me. The life of the mind, *bah!*" Of course, reading was the most private of activities. In the early days, she had tried taking out of the library the books he was reading and sitting beside him with her identical book in hand. But she found books boring. "And what about you," he'd retorted, "your life is just a constant wanting. First this outfit, then that one. This hair color than that. You're a walking commercial."

When they were both in tears, she said how lonely she was. "Before I hate you and you hate me, let me go. I want to do *something!*"

"I'm not holding you, so go, but Phyllis stays."

"But I'm her mother!"

Panic hit the back of his throat, as he threatened her with a court battle, knowing that if she agreed to fight it out with Phyllis a pawn between them, he'd have given up. But Allison had always been intimidated by his courtroom experience. Finally, her mouth a bitter line, she gave him custody, with liberal visiting rights during the summers, which she kept up for the first two years, then lost a summer when she spent it traveling through Europe with her wealthy new husband. The next year the visit was shortened when Phyllis woke him in the middle of the night, calling from the "scary house" where she pretended to be asleep while the babysitter talked to her boyfriend and watched TV in a distant room.

"I think there's somebody outside, Dad. What should I do?" He told her to call 911 and then to call him right back. When five minutes had passed, he called her and waited through the sixth ring before someone finally picked up. Immediately the line went dead, and he called 911 himself, waiting anxiously until Phyllis called and said, "I'm okay, Dad, I guess it was nothing," while the babysitter scolded her in the background. Two days later she was on a plane for home, and the summer visits dwindled to trips to Australia, Ireland, and Russia, and a week-long visit during Christmas break, to their home. It was heady stuff, and it usually took Phyllis several days to wind down. She spoke cheerfully with her mother every few weeks, and on her birthday and Mother's Day, sweet cards proclaimed, "Mommy, you're the best!"

They settled into their life together. She liked to read as much as he did, loved for him to read to her, but she also enjoyed exploring the woods, alone except for Veronica, who padded along after her as if she were a dog. Patrick promised himself he would help her create a mind that knew no imaginative bounds, one that could read the world and fashion a place in it. Bedtime would be a time for sharing—as his own childhood bedtimes had been. He promised himself he would put her first. He would lay down the book. If he were on the phone, he'd put his hand over the phone to hear what Phyllis had to say.

Even on difficult days, when she had perfected the silent treatment, stunning him with her contempt, once she settled into her bed, smelling of soap, her pillow propped against his hip, she was rapt. The stories he told and the books he read always lasted several nights, even weeks, and he'd say at the close of a night's reading, "But that is nothing compared to what I will tell you tomorrow night," and she soon began finishing the line, "if only you will spare me tonight." Until recently, she hadn't let him slip away without a sleepy hug and a mumbled "night-night." Now she was out within minutes, her weight sinking away from him as her shoulders softened into slumber.

He set bacon and eggs on a plate. "Phyl? Saturday Special, two bits!"

She picked up two red poker chips from the bowl on the counter and dropped them into a jar marked "Patrick." Their system of paying in poker chips for good deeds let them see in bright, rattling colors who needed to help out more, or who had a day off coming.

"You got any shopping in town today?" she asked.

She looked forward to their Saturday shopping ritual, and he frequently found sugary and salty packages slipped into their shopping cart. They always ran into someone they knew, and increasingly Phyllis seemed to be on the look-out. "Oh, there's Jenny. She's a snot." Or, "There's that new kid Sonny. He's kinda cute, isn't he," slipping behind Patrick, "Don't let him see me!"

On this day, he knew something was up when he emerged from the meat section and saw her slip out of the grocery store. Later, as he wheeled the cart into the parking lot, she reappeared with a bag from the pharmacy next door.

"Whatcha got there?" he asked as he started the car.

"That's my secret." She glared at him. "Can't I even go birthday shopping without you snooping around?" His birthday was still three weeks away, but he let it go.

When they got home and had unpacked groceries, she went up to her bathroom and changed. "I'm going for a walk!" she called on her way out.

Patrick looked up in time to see Veronica's gray bush of a tail as she slipped out the door behind Phyllis.

II

She had five forts, some built with Patrick's help, others by her own persistent labor. Now she paused near one, her eyes searching the dried leaves. She found a sturdy looking stick and tore at the tip until it was pointed enough to dig with. She flicked away the dried leaves, and Veronica scrambled after them. Phyllis pressed the point into the soft, loose earth and dug until she could fit her hand into the hole. She looked back toward home, then opened the bag and pulled out the folded pad wrapped in toilet paper. When she had covered it and stomped it down, she sprinkled leaves over the mound. Veronica patted them.

Over the next hill, a few minutes away, lay the sandstone quarry. Phyllis had been there twice with Patrick. He didn't like her to come near it, but no harm in taking a quick look. The quarry was long deserted, the hang-out of trouble-makers, a place for teenagers to make out. An old gravel road followed her side of the quarry. It was blocked at the entrance, but people drove through the weeds and potholes on either side of the barricade. Beyond the road, the quarry plunged to its treacherous depths. She had heard it was over four hundred feet deep in places, though any large number would have impressed her. She liked to look at it from a distance, imagining the gravity of all that soundless space pulling her toward the bottom. She loved the mixture of horror and awe she felt whenever nature turned ominous—like the waves in Australia, taller than her school, that swallowed surfers then spat them out in gray curls and crashes of white foam. It was her secret desire to watch from a ditch when a tornado passed over. Last summer when she and Patrick had gone to Niagara Falls, she'd felt hypnotized by the deep green rushing water. Even though a fence separated her from certain death, she felt pulled toward it. She'd asked endless questions about the man who went down in a barrel and survived. Did he wear padding? Did the barrel break open on the rocks? Could this be an example of a real miracle? In a recurrent dream she rushed over the edge of the great falls, curled in a cardboard box.

She stood at the edge of the woods. She could see the far walls of the great oval where several black circles, probably shallow caves, seemed tattooed on the surface. Here and there a tree or a bush had taken root and grown upward toward the rim.

Veronica trotted in front of her, her gray body dwarfed by the gaping hole beyond.

"Veronica, you come back here!" she called then hurried after her and grabbed her. A few more steps and she'd be close enough to see the bottom. She could feel her father's eyes watching her as she peered over the edge, at a jumble of big boulders interspersed with stagnant pools and cattails growing at the edges. The giant hole emitted a dusty, silent belch.

"Well, if it isn't Miss Priss."

She whirled around. Vince and Kevin and Doober walked toward her. A partial six-pack of beer dangled from Doober's fingertips and a cigarette from his lips. Vince and Kevin each held a beer. They separated when they saw her look toward the woods, each moving silently, signaling their intentions with a nod and a flick of the wrist.

"And she's got a pussy cat with her. I like cats. Can I hold her?" Doober's low voice slipped out of the sides of his mouth. He stepped forward as the other two circled behind her. Now she stood in the center of their triangle. She held tight to Veronica and kept her eyes on Doober. From behind, Vince shoved her so that she stumbled and loosened her grip on Veronica. Doober snatched her away.

"Oh, this is a pretty cat. Is he yours? Do you care if I keep him for a while?"

She twisted away from Kevin, whose chin was hooked over her shoulder. She could smell beer as he reached around and grabbed her breast.

"Oh, she's got 'em," he hooted, "She's got 'em all right."

"Course she's got 'em, you idiot. She's a woman, ain't ya, Pill-is," Vince's voice went silky in her other ear, and she spun around to face him.

"That's none of your business!"

He imitated her, elbows out, chanting in a high, squeaky voice, "None of your business, none of your business."

"We can make it our business. You like your cat a lot, don't you?" Doober waited. She reached for Veronica, but he stepped back.

"Well, do you?"

She nodded.

"Then you take off your clothes and I won't throw him into the quarry."

Kevin spoke low, as if he was telling her a secret, "You know, their brains explode before they hit the bottom, so you don't have to worry about him getting bruised when his body bounces off the rocks." He slapped a high-five with Vince.

"Just let me go home." She knew they'd make her words sound ridiculous.

Doober started walking toward the edge but stopped as Phyllis bent down and pulled off her sneakers. She couldn't see them through a blur of tears, though she could hear their breathing as they gathered around her.

"Now take your training bra off," Doober said.

"Look at all those dimples." Kevin pushed his finger into her stomach. She slapped his hand away.

"Ooohh," they squealed and slapped at each other's wrists.

She wondered if she could signal Veronica to bite Doober, then grab her and run, but Doober's arms looked like tree roots growing around a gray cloud. Veronica stared at her with angry, black eyes. Phyllis shook her legs so her pants would slide over her ankles, set them neatly beside her, and stood up, her arms crossed over her chest. She looked into Doober's glinting eyes and shook her head slowly when he nodded toward her underwear. He grabbed Veronica behind her neck and held her above his head so her eyes became slits.

"Why are you so mean?" she cried and grabbed at Doober's arm.

"Why are you so stupid? Take 'em off, like I said."

Numbness crept up her arms as she fumbled with her underwear. She watched her hands shake as if they belonged to someone else.

"Gross!"

"Gag me! That's disgusting!" Kevin and Vince fell to the ground, pretending to throw up and flinging stones over their heads. Then Kevin picked up a branch that lay nearby, and holding it as far from himself as he could and pinching his nose, he picked up her underwear and the new sanitary pad and tossed them over the edge. The rest of her clothes followed. Her sweatshirt filled with air for a moment, looking foolish and fat, before it plummeted out of sight.

"Give me my cat now," she said, reaching for her, but Doober shook his head and she let her hands drop to her sides, then lifted them again and crossed her breasts.

"Go down on me," he ordered, and when she didn't move, "Suck me first." She had heard of couples making out so much that they sucked each other's skin and made dark marks around their necks. She looked at him, puzzled. He handed Veronica to Kevin and beckoned to his pants.

"Undo them."

"No."

"Undo them."

"No, I-I can't."

"Kevin, pitch the cat."

"Nooo."

He pushed her to her knees. She fumbled with his pants until he pushed her hands away and unzipped them himself. She closed her eyes then opened them in alarm when she felt her throat forced open. Dark hairs in a straight line divided his stomach in half before they emerged as stiff snarls that smelled like a chicken coop. Stones jabbed in her knees.

"You boys want to be next?"

Her cheek lay in a cushion of gravel where Doober had pushed her, and when she opened her eyes she saw his big toes pushing out of his tennis shoes and at the same time it seemed to her that she could also see Kevin, though he was surely behind her now, looking down at her and shaking his head. Her vision shifted to Vince as he turned away and said, "I don't know. She's in our homeroom. She could get us in trouble."

"Not if she's scared enough. Hey, girl! Look here!" Phyllis sat up in time to see him grab Veronica from Kevin's arms and walk quickly toward the edge. She lunged toward him, grabbing the cuff of his jeans, so that as he released the cat and as Phyllis's body fell hard against the gravel, Veronica twisted, claws extended, and raked his forearm. Then she was gone.

For a moment Phyllis heard the cat's cry, then it stopped, abruptly, as if someone had slammed a door on it, or as if the bottom had rushed up to meet her. Phyllis felt something inside her stomach rip loose, forcing her mouth open. She screamed, took a breath, and screamed again. The quarry walls resounded, and the two boys stared in alarm, their hands over their ears. It was Doober who finally swung toward her, clutching his torn arm in rage and pain, as the back of his fist caught her chin. "Shut up, bitch!" She stumbled back over a branch and fell, her hand closing over it as though she had only just remembered what it was for. In the next motion, she regained her balance and brought the branch up into his face. He fell back, his hands to his temple. For a moment, just before the gush of blood leaped across his face, everyone froze.

"I'm getting the hell out of here," Kevin cried. "Come on, dudes, let's leave this FAT STUPID GIRL and get the hell out of here."

Vince started after him, then stopped when Doober struggled to his feet, whimpering, "Jesus Christ, my eyes! I can't see!"

They heard the car at the same moment.

"Come on, man, let's get out of here. Someone's coming."

Bracing Doober with one hand, Vince led them toward the far end of the quarry, where they disappeared into the woods. Phyllis dropped to her knees and her head fell forward. She could feel the gravel gouging into her knees, but the pain seemed far away, like a dim light.

"Hey, girl, you all right? Hey, Sonny, you know her?"

Someone pulled at her arm. She lifted her head and grasped the stick tightly, jabbing it at them.

"Get away, get away, get away."

"Okay, okay," he said and backed up. "You know her, Sonny?"

"Her name's Phyllis Shaw."

"Patrick Shaw's kid?"

Phyllis looked toward the form that had said her father's name.

"You stay here," it was saying to the boy, "so nothing happens. Get the blanket out of the trunk first. I'll go get her old man."

A violent trembling shot across her shoulders, then down her sides and into her legs. Her teeth rattled. When Sonny stretched out his arm to offer her the blanket, she tightened her grip on the branch and pointed it toward him. He stepped back.

"Hey, I just want to give you this." He turned his face away as he held the blanket toward her, then edged near enough for her to reach it, and dropped it.

When he stepped away and stood with his back to her, she grabbed the blanket and fumbled with it until she had draped it around her shoulders.

She stood, and now they were side by side but facing different directions, separated by a few feet of gravel. She could hear him snapping something, a twig maybe, as she looked toward the quarry. There was only that small *snap, snap* beside her and in front of her a silence that boiled over the rim of the quarry, like a hot breath, as though some bottom dweller (a term that always made her and Kelly laugh) had been awakened. As if he had been climbing the invisible wall and now waited just an arm's length from the edge. Chills moved up her spine, raising goose bumps on her arms.

"You're lucky we came by." Then, "That was stupid." She listened for what he would say next. "I guess your dad will be here soon." He seemed to be waiting for her to say something, but then he went on, "I'm real sorry whatever happened."

Tears formed, and their eyes met for a moment.

She stumbled, but he didn't follow, or if he did, she couldn't hear him. And when the shady cool of the woods surrounded her, she stopped and leaned against a tree. The sun hovered over the far rim of the quarry, sending rose-colored shadows into the woods around her. She looked down at a line of blood zigzagging toward her ankle, then her legs started shaking again, so she turned and ran on.

In their yard, she paused. Patrick was calling for her from the front. She made a dash for the back door, tried to stop it from slamming, and hurried through the hallway and up the stairs to the bathroom. She locked the door and went to the tub and turned on both faucets full blast. She stepped in. A blue plastic cup had been left on the drain and now it sent water spattering everywhere. She watched it, wondering why it didn't budge with all that water plowing down on it. Eventually it popped away. She adjusted the temperature and stepped in. The water turned gray, then a line of red bubbled up. She quickly swished the water so that it all blended into a messy brown, topped with a filmy layer.

Why had she let her go so easily? Veronica had tried to tell her with her great, round eyes to do *something,* to get her out of those arms that tried to squeeze the breath right out of her.

Tapping on the door made her sit up and wipe her face.

"Phyllis?"

"Go away."

"Please." His voice cracked like it always did when he got emotional, and she could hear him try to change it so it would sound normal. "Ned just drove up, said he saw you by the quarry. Was that you?"

She didn't answer.

He was silent a moment. "Phyllis. Please."

She stood up and wrapped the beach towel around herself then let him in. He lowered himself to the toilet while she studied a square of tile that had been chipped in the corner and was now filled with lint and dirt. When he reached for her hand, she let him pull her into his lap. His smell was warm and familiar, and she buried her face in his shoulder. When he pulled away to look at her, his eyes were red.

"What happened?"

"They killed Veronica, Daddy, they killed her."

He smoothed her hair and whispered, "Did somebody hurt you, Phyllis?"

She shook her head.

"Ned said you were naked."

This made tears fill her eyes.

"It's okay to tell me. I need to know what happened. What happened?"

"You don't understand!"

"What don't I understand, Phyl?"

"They . . . threw . . . her . . . over the edge."

When she stood, a drop of blood landed on one of the tiles between her feet.

"You're bleeding," he said, his voice hard. "Did anyone—?"

"I started my period." Clutching the towel around her, she opened the cupboard beneath the washbasin and took a sanitary napkin out of the box and handed it to him.

Taking it, he whispered, "I didn't—you didn't—"

"It's no big deal."

He handed it back to her. "I'll go wait in your room for you."

When she had crawled under the covers and faced the wall, he sat behind her.

"I love you, honey."

She nodded.

"Will you tell me what happened?"

She shook her head.

"I need to know. It's important."

"Something's not right," she said. "If I were falling over a cliff, I would scream all the way to the bottom."

"I don't understand."

She sat up. "Dad. I want to go back to the quarry."

"What are you talking about?"

"I know you won't believe me, but I think Veronica's waiting for me."

She turned the covers back and threw her legs over the edge.

"Phyllis. We can't go out there now. In the morning at least you could see."

"When we first got there, just me and her, I was looking at the other side and there are little caves and some of them have trees growing around the openings. And when Doober—

"When he threw Veronica over the edge, I grabbed his leg and he slipped a little. He didn't throw her as far as he meant to, and then she scratched his arm and went over the edge. But she went just over the edge, you know? Just barely, not out into the air."

She jumped up. "And I even saw her clawing the air a little before she caught sight of me. And I know she's waiting for me to get her. I know it!"

He took her arm and turned her around.

"If I do this for you . . . if I take you out there, will you at least think about telling me what happened?"

She pulled on her shoes. "Yes, yes, *come on!*" She got to the car first and got in, then looked through the window, as the moon eased above the tree line, pulling wisps of cloud with it.

The hood became a shimmering plate as the headlights pointed the way.

"Who's this Doober you mentioned?"

"He's in my school. It was him and Vince and Kevin Brady. They made me take off my clothes and he made me . . ." He leaned toward her to hear. "He said if I didn't suck him he'd throw Veronica over the edge. And then he threw her over anyway!"

He clutched the steering wheel. "Goddammit. Goddammit!" His left fist slammed the window beside him.

"Dad, you're scaring me."

He put both hands back on the wheel. "And he's got scratch marks on arm?"

"Not only that," she said, "I clubbed him over the head with a big stick and he ran away with blood all over him."

"So, he won't be hard to recognize."

"Dad, don't do anything stupid. You're not the macho type."

He paused at the gated barricade. The moon seemed stuck in the tree line beside them. She pointed, "Just drive around on that side." Gravel crunched beneath the tires.

"Here we are," she said, "there's the branch."

They each carried a flashlight, but before they had walked more than a few feet toward the edge, they heard Veronica's deep cry. It crawled up the side of the cliff and filled the bowl of the quarry, as if it were the voice of night itself.

"There she is! I told you!"

"I'll be damned."

Her eyes flashed yellow some six feet below them where she clung to a small bush.

"Wait here," he said, "I'm going to see if we can get a branch for her to climb up."

"There's one right there. It really comes in handy."

"Shine your light down there so we can see if there's a place I can lodge this. Even if I do," he added, "It's a sure bet she won't want to let go of that bush she's on."

"How about right there?" Phyllis gestured with her flashlight.

"Okay, I'll try wedging it in a bit."

Veronica reached a hesitant paw toward the log. She meowed once, a questioning voice, then reached out with her other paw and pulled herself out of the crouching position. She started to climb but paused part way up.

"Don't shine in her eyes, Phyl. Point your light to the ground beside me."

She scurried up, gripping the branch, then stopped a foot from the edge. Phyllis leaned forward and Patrick grabbed her leg.

"I've got her!"

Patrick stood and gave the branch a push. They listened to the crackle of brush breaking and the muffled thud. Now the quarry rang with silence.

When they got home, Phyllis set out a bowl of food and some water, before climbing back into bed.

"I really bashed him hard, Dad." She lay back on her pillow, her eyes closed.

"I want you to know something," he said. "What happened tonight was dead wrong. It's not supposed to be like that. But there are a lot of bad people, bad men. I haven't done a very good job of preparing you, have I?"

"I know all about it from school, Dad. Really. I just didn't know it was so disgusting."

She patted his knee. "I'll be okay." Veronica had climbed into his lap and her claws made rasping sounds against his jeans.

"Don't do anything stupid, Dad."

"What kind of stupid thing do you think I'd do?"

"I don't know, it's just that, well, I already took care of it. Those guys don't scare me. I'll be okay, as long as he didn't give me the clap or something."

He didn't answer, though she could hear him grinding his teeth. She closed her eyes and after a while felt herself drifting. She roused herself enough to say, "Do you think cats ever think about what if?"

"I don't know."

After he'd left, she heard his voice on the phone downstairs. She could imagine herself creeping down the stairs to listen. She woke when front door lock clicked. From the window where she knelt, she saw him get into the car. In the rear window, the captured moon pressed itself against the glass and looked up at her. He closed the door but did not turn on the headlights. The moon had escaped and now, with the stars, shown down on a silvery fish that disappeared into the dark mouth of the trees. For a few moments, the stars pulsed, then the car lights emerged further down the road as he headed toward town.

Don't Say Maybe

If you've never had to get around this hilly campus in a wheel-chair, I don't want to hear about there's no parking. If it's not roots buckling the concrete, it's grounds people blocking portions under repair. Half the time on the Hill I drive in the street, go ahead and lay on your horn. I know sign language.

I live on Chestnut Street, four blocks from campus and just a few doors down from Ms. Terrell, who is teaching the women's studies class I'm in. Hey, it meets a gen-ed requirement. First day I did the class demographics: thirteen blondes, eight brunettes, one redhead, and one kinkyhead. Twenty-two are able-bodied, one is not. It's an affirmative action dream come true. By my guidelines, we have three obese, seven getting close (chips, little debbies before class), and five paperclips. We have two guys, and they're working on their six-packs and taking this class to pick up chicks. The blonde one says this. I sidle my eyes to the teacher.

I say, "My name is Shamari, I grew up in Louisville, and I'm taking this class for the same reason she is." I point to Molly, who has just introduced herself as the president of the LGBTQ group on campus, saying, "I don't think most people have thought much about how gender affects the world, me included, and I want to find out." That sounded pretty good to me, though the rules are pretty simple, aren't they? Like everything else, there's the have-a-lots and the not-haves and we all have our job to do, making life for the other half as difficult as possible. Maybe the have-somes round things out. Or, maybe they're the meanest ones.

Someone asks what LGBTQ stands for and when she hears the answer says oh like an escaping fart. The blond guy says, "We don't have any transsexuals on this campus, do we? Please say no."

LG cuts him a look. "I know two. One's a performer in Nashville and she's great."

"Well, I think it's sick," he says, "I don't care how good they can lip sync."

"Sick is a state of mind," she flashes then says maybe this class will correct some people's stereotypes. He mutters "dyke" for his half of the class to hear. Something in my head goes, Hmm. Ms. Terrell says, "Issues of sexuality and identity are part of what this class is about, and I'm glad to see we've got students willing to say what they think, but we need to be open-minded and accepting of difference." Then she goes on to lay out a few rules for conduct, and things settle down. Keywords: respect, don't interrupt, open your mind.

She keeps us the whole time, which doesn't seem quite sporting, but most of my professors aren't. By the time I get out of the building, the crowd has thinned and I make my way to my next class, cussing when the back wheel catches the edge of the sidewalk and pulls me into the grass. Not to worry. I drive an Extreme 4x4, the beemer of wheelchairs.

On the way home, I think about how Ms. Terrell started the class with the terms *demographics* and *subtext.* "From an early age, we all learn to read between the lines. Sometimes it's a matter of survival. Sometimes it's about hanging on to power. I want you to think about the subtext of your own life. Get underneath the demographics."

So, for our in-class writing assignment, I say how I was born in Louisville, dot, dot, dot, but if you assume I grew up in the west end, that's where you need to look *underneath.* In the east end, we've got cars in garages, an occasional swimming pool, and college on the horizon. My mom wanted my brother and me to come to Western, because she did. We're so upwardly mobile, it's dizzying. Like Tracy Chapman says, "Here in subcity, life is hard." Only I say, "Here in *suburbcity,* life is *something else.*" I don't pretend to know the answer.

I used to wish I had grown up in Shawnee Park, where liquor stores come every other corner and are long and dark, and tough black kids grow up begging their fathers (if they're around) for change, fifty cents a huff. Da'shay, who is a friend from high school, invited me over a couple of times. Shawnee Park, where loud, skinny girls or loud, fat girls walk four deep and you hafta step offa de damn sidewalk less you wanna wake up wit yo face smiling achoo from de dark side a yo ass. That's a direct quote. Her mother got her right out of there and into one of the magnet schools, where I was going. The first time we met I corrected something one of the girls she was standing with said. She looked me up and down with her truly black eyes and said, "Look like we got a cracker think she gonna tell us what it gonna be."

"She a cracker, I'ma cracka too, ho," says Da'shay, then she grabs the handles of my chair and we rocket outta there. She's one of them so she can get away with that kinda shit.

There are so many subtexts I get dizzy. Can you have a subtext to the subtext? Maybe it's better to just look at the damn text and forget sub. Shamari, computer programming student. Shamari, black girl in a wheelchair. Shamari, she looking out the window at people walking by. The room is dark, the streetlights bright. Music pours over her shoulder and into the night. Sometimes people look up, but they don't see. Shamari, she somewhere round here.

Make Me Wanna Holler

Our assignment is to research a famous woman from the 20th century. We are supposed to do this all online, and in pairs put together a PowerPoint presentation. Ms. Terrell is going to let the five best present theirs to the class. We get fifteen minutes to share ideas and pick who we're going to work with. I mention that I'd like to do Etta James and then have to explain that she's a great R&B singer, and that gets everyone else throwing out names of female singers. Presley Palmer (aka Pissy Pants—I nicknamed her last semester when we were in English 300 together) says no one's made a bigger impact than Madonna, so that's who she's going to work on with her sorority sister, Tina the Trying Twin (T the TT or just Triple T for short). I watch everyone pair up, thinking I'm going to have to pay somebody, when LG pulls up a desk next to mine.

When she sits down, her blue jeans, which are tight, show her legs to be extremely muscular. Two holes open up over her knees like smiles. A long white string over her right knee breaks and the two ends join the rest of the fringe. She doesn't notice.

She grips the edge of her desk, tapping with her thumbs. "I like your idea. Do you care if I work on it with you?"

"You'll have to get in line."

I feel a twinge in my stomach when she laughs. Like what happens on a cold day when you take your first sip of coffee, and you feel it go all the way down, real slow. No, more like brandy—that slow hot spread in your stomach rushing up to your brain, where dormant cells say, hey, girl, did you feel that?

She sticks her hand out, and since my good hand is my left one, when I put it in hers, it's like we're holding hands. I learned long ago that people will do just about anything to avoid gripping my right hand in theirs.

"So why do you want to do Etta James? You're a white girl."

"Is it that obvious?" She gets a worried look as she stares at her arms.

"Well, you're pretty tan."

"I work at a barn. University horse barn. I have horses. You like horses?"

I notice she says the word *horses* a lot. "No, I do not," I say firmly. "I like animals that can't look down on you. I prefer to look down on them."

"Well, once you're riding, that's what you do. Mostly the back of their neck and ears."

"That doesn't count."

She shrugs, and we get down to the business of our project. It turns out she has three of her CDs—and a record, get this, of *Etta James Rocks the House,* recorded live in Nashville.

"Hey, if you want, I can burn a CD of that—one for you and one for me, of course."

"You can make a CD from a record?" She sounds like I did when I first learned that the Pledge of Allegiance didn't always say "under God."

I reassure her that with technology anything is possible, and as everyone's heading out of the building like busy ants with cell phones for antennae, she says, "Can I give you a lift?"

"Nah, it's all downhill from here."

That's when I remember I have another class and hightail it back to Cherry Hall.

Long Line of Don't Mean Maybe

I'm in trouble. That night after I crawl into bed, I put on Roberta real low and get to know myself. My brain refuses to empty itself of Molly's crooked smile and long legs. I have a thing for legs, probably because mine are so crazy. You know how some branches have a big ball growing on them? That's my legs. Skinny, skinny, with knees like tree burls. Legs can be so beautiful, and when they're strong legs, I just about can't look away. I love those two little lines at the back of knees. I'll bet hers are long and straight.

I can't afford to lose sleep like this. My cells are eight-hours-a-night-dependent. Two mornings a week, I have to get up early and work at the computer lab from 8:00 till 2:00, and I also work two nights a week. If I'm the least bit tired, I can hardly make it to my first potty break. It's that boring. And the students! *My computer screen's blank.* Try turning on the monitor. *My computer just froze.* Try closing about fifteen of those twenty windows. *What's my password?* I just hold up my hand in the shape of an L on my forehead. Sometimes they laugh.

For some reason work is a breeze. My supervisor even calls me chatty.

In class I pull a desk next to my chair, like I usually do, so I have something to write on. Molly doesn't bat an eye when she comes in but sits down between me and Pissy Pants. Ms. Terrell is passing something out, and when PP hands the pile to Molly, she gives her a big smile, and for the rest of the class I keep my eye on them, which isn't so easy, till I roll back a little and can see the backs of their heads. Blond and shiny and looking like a commercial for Nice 'n Easy next to brown and glossy—wait a minute, is that a little piece of hay stuck in there? I reach over and pluck it out. Molly feels the tug and turns around. I hold it out to her like it's a little bouquet as the cells in my face imitate a tomato.

"There it is!" she says. PP sees me pass her the straw and leans over and says something. Molly just shrugs. I spend the next ten minutes imagining what she said, so I don't hear when I get called on.

"Umm," is what comes out as I burrow my eyes into the pages like the answer is in a pop-up window under someone's yellow highlighting. I hear PP giggle behind her hand and then Molly whispers out of the corner of her mouth, "Tell her how Etta James is a feminist."

"Well," I say, "she probably wouldn't have called herself that."

"Did she have an overall message, do you think? Since our reading is on blues women, I thought you might see Etta James fitting into what Davis is saying here."

"She comes from a long line of don't mean maybe," I say. "I guess that's feminist." A few people snicker and discussion moves on (respectfully) to something else.

That night Don't-Mean-Maybe calls to check on me. Mom didn't want me to live alone, wanted me to join Alpha Kappa Alpha, her sorority. I put in a good-faith effort (okay, maybe not), but I didn't like the girls. Da'shay's an exception. She says, "They support unity among black women," but when I tell her it's only *some* black women they want to unity with, she punches me and says, "Oooh, you're hostile, girl." She pretends there's something under the surface. The ones I saw prancing around only cared how their asses looked in their shorts. I *know* these girls, mean as snakes if you want to know the truth. They have a Miss Black Western pageant every year that brings them out of the woodwork. It's embarrassing. I told Da'shay if she ever runs for queen I'll never speak to her again, but she says, "You're just jealous cuz you don't think you'd stand a chance." That's her explanation for everything. Her boyfriend smacking her around? He's just jealous. He really loves her. She makes me want say, "Not everyone wants what the next guy has. Some people care about bigger issues." But she'd just laugh, "That's what they *say,* but it's not what they *mean.*" Or maybe, "Hey, we're all about world peace."

Mom wants to make sure I haven't fallen and hit my head open or gotten hit by a car or drowned in the bathtub or raped by one of the many men stalking me or burned my leg without knowing it. I have some feeling in my legs, so when I got second degree burns once, it was a part that's dead asleep, and it was the smell that alerted me. I reassure her that my social calendar is about to burst and she says they'll see me at Thanksgiving and we hang up. There are some things my mother wouldn't understand, and one of them is me and women. She once said, when she found me playing in bed with my best friend, "Shamari, just because you're crippled doesn't mean you have to lower your expectations." Anyone who's ever had a mother knows they have the most efficient means for cutting you open. Slice and dice Mom.

When it was obvious the medical profession couldn't fix me, despite a vigorous program of physical therapy that helped but didn't put things back the way they were, she started taking me to faith healers, mostly in Kentucky, but as far away as South Carolina and Georgia. It's amazing how a desperate black woman with money makes healers out of crooks. We were supposed to go up to Cincinnati the day I couldn't take it anymore. I put on my brakes, she undid them, I locked them again, our fingers clawing at each other. She reached back to smack me and my brother stepped in and grabbed her hand.

"Don't hit Shamari," he said, and it's the last time I saw him in tears.

"Then maybe I need to hit you." She realigned her arm, ready to backhand him, but something in his face stopped her. She turned back to me, her voice high and pinching, "I just want you to be whole, baby, that's all I want. I just want you to be whole again."

Snot ran down my face. "I'm all here," I screamed, "I just can't walk anymore."

She clamped her hands over her mouth. "Oh, sweet Jesus," she cried, "forgive me. Shamari, you know what I mean. You know that's not what I think."

My dad walked in from getting the car loaded and saw Mom falling back on the sofa and Tyrone wiping his eyes with his sleeves, me trying to catch my breath. "Did I miss something?" he asks. "We're not going anywhere," she said. "Just forget the whole thing." She got up and walked upstairs. That night she put cornrows in my hair while we all sat around eating popcorn and watching *Kings of Comedy.*

I hold it like a little light in my heart, the time my mom apologized and cried for something hard she said to me.

I need a Sunday kind of love

Three weeks later, we decide we can get our presentation done if we meet on Sunday at my apartment. People who don't live in a wheelchair are usually curious about practical matters, like how do I get into the cabinets above the counters or how do I use the toilet. I have one word for them, Heave-ho. I can stand, leaning against the counters, so I can reach the same as anyone, I just do it a little quicker. My right hand is missing two fingers but I've got my thumb, which is a blessing, as my mom would say. If I use the stove, that means I'm cooking at eye-level, so I usually set the electric skillet on the table and cook there. Baking is also easier, so I make some cookies and put on a pot of strong coffee.

She comes right on time and takes a look around my apartment, her hands in her pockets and her brown ponytail brushing her back. She takes in my computer table and my programming homework in a dozen haphazard stacks of books, paper, and CDs.

"Welcome to my world."

"Nice place. I love these old houses."

"It's old all right, old and leaky, and the floors in the apartment above me creak whenever they go to the bathroom. You want a cookie?"

She takes a big bite. Three inches from my face her jeans say Chic. She eats the other half then rubs her tongue over her teeth. I do the same, like I'm a mirror. Chocolate nestles in the corners of her lips. "How are my teeth?" she asks, and when I shake my head, she rubs them some more with her tongue (a voice in my head says *here, let me do that),* then she gives up and goes to the bathroom.

I roll over to my computer, which is on a big table where we can both sit and look at the screen. We browse for an hour or so, hitting a number of fan sites, lyrics, posters, memorabilia for sale, biographies, and lots of pictures of Etta with a microphone, getting fatter through the years. We look at the concerts coming up, but the nearest one is in Pennsylvania and already sold out. We make a string of cuts, from Etta grunting to Etta belting it out loud and clear. Using Flash, I make it seem like there are two Ettas, young Etta and old Etta, singing back and forth.

"No one else is going to be able to touch this, you know?" Her eyes glisten. "I could never have done anything this good on my own. I'd have had a couple of clunky old slides and then there'd be a blank one that I couldn't explain."

About 10:00 I bring out the big bottle of Courvoisier I got for my birthday last year. We decide to broaden our research by listening to other blues and soul queens, "for context," LG says, so we play Dionne, Aretha, Roberta, Koko. We sing, "You make me feel like a natural woman" so loud my neighbors pound on the wall. At 11:30, we finish popping the images, animated gifs, and text into place. She leans back and her shirt pulls tight over her breasts, which are little enough she doesn't have to wear a bra. She puts her hands behind her head and her biceps pop (I like arms, too, though I have to say that mine are pretty nice).

"How tall are you anyway?"

"Six feet. Tall for a girl, I know. How 'bout you?"

"Most of the time four feet or so."

She smiles. "So how did it happen?"

I hold up my right hand and say, "Birth defect," and point to my legs and say, "Swimming pool."

"Did you dive into the shallow end?"

"It was the deep end, but not as deep as I thought. I was fourteen and spent the summer playing in a neighbor's pool, then went to another friend's house and dove in thinking it was nine feet like my neighbor's but it wasn't."

"Was someone there with you?"

"My friend. When I came up doing the dead man's float, she ran and got her parents and they pulled me out. Ambulance. Lights, sirens. Surgery. I had headaches for a while. My muscles spasm if they get tired."

"Tough luck."

"Yeah, if it wasn't for bad luck . . ." She smiles at the Etta reference.

"Seeing as how I want to work with big animals for the rest of my life, it would kill me. You're good at computers, where it doesn't matter if you're confined to a wheelchair."

I sigh. "Two things you need to know, Molly. I got interested in computers *after* this happened, when I started being stuck at home while my friends ran around. I was in track *before* this happened, computers *after.* Second, *confined* is not what I'd call it."

She grimaces then hits her forehead. "Sorry for being stuck in my own narrow world."

"Well, you can't know everything, after all." I can be very forgiving.

She leans in close and says, "You don't know how pretty you are, do you," like it's not really a question. Screensaver Etta is hitting herself in the head with her microphone, fascinated, and I manage to slur out, "I guess I know what I need to know."

"I'll bet you do." She stands, and I figure this is her way of calling it a night, but she starts swaying her hips and then pulls my chair around. "Can you stand?" I shake my head no, then shrug and hold my thumb and finger apart about an inch. Before I know it, she's reached down and pulled me up. "Stand on my feet," she says and helps me position my toes on hers. All my weight is against her, my heart slamming. Etta sings, "I need a Sunday kind of love," and Molly's doing backup in my ear.

She takes my right hand and holds it in hers, our arms out straight, so now she's supporting me with one arm gripping me around my waist.

"Aren't I getting heavy?" I ask, like I'm being considerate, but in truth I just couldn't stand to be the one who wants to keep going if she's had enough, but she mumbles, "uh-uh."

Etta starts singing "Now you said I'm only holding you down, like some old rock you been dragging around." I laugh when she says, "Yes, I'm your rock, and I'm rolling away." She starts giggling, too, and then she stumbles and down we go. "Come back here, Rock," she says when I start rolling away. I prop myself on my elbows and watch her eyes soften and her hair swirl where it's come loose in the back. I inch toward her and touch her lips. She grips the back of my neck and pulls me on top, and her tongue reaches back to last week, where I can almost hear lonely old me getting sucked into the here and now.

Don't open the door to heaven if I can't come in

It's no contest. Etta gets first prize. Other students come up to us with compliments, and when they ask how we got the images to move, Molly nods to me. Even old PP says we did a great job. Molly keeps sitting between us, but she acts as if nothing happened, so I keep my cool. A few weeks go by where all we say is hi how ya doin. I begin to see that maybe what happened wasn't such a big deal for her. I begin to worry.

It's November suddenly and getting harder to make small talk. My answers get shorter and I start pretending I didn't see her wave. One day, I'm sitting outside the Java House, eating a slice of pizza and slurping down a big Coke, when I see her come down the steps, rubbing shoulders with Presley. A big ball of greasy cheese pauses on the way down. I jerk the *College Herald* up over my face (which is stupid as my chair isn't what you'd call easy to miss). When I peek around the edge of the paper, they're heading away, and I know in my heart of hearts that they're going to her sorority dorm to make sweet, able-bodied love. I really do not need that particular image in my head.

Now, I am one tough cookie, that's how my mother raised me. And she's from the same line of don't mean maybe that Etta is. My mom may be vice president for a big insurance company, but her subtext is redneck Kentucky, which she ran away from to south side Chicago, where my dad fell in love with her voice when he called to buy some insurance at a rinky-dink office and then whisked her back to Kentucky, only this time Louisville, where they nickel and dimed it through law school for him and MBA for her. No one talks better English than my mom, but once we're home, it's *Don't let me see you feelin' sorry for yourself, else I give you somethin' to be sorry about. You stick that lip out any further, you gonna trip on it. You give a white person a inch, they see you to the river. Never knew a white boy (or girl?) do anything with a black girl that wasn't dirty. If you's white, you all right, brown you gonna get down, but if you's black, you better git back.*

You give it enough subtext, even a tough cookie gonna crumble, so before that happens here in front of witnesses, this cookie's gonna roll out de do'. I wheel the long way around the library and up the hill on State Street, then since traffic's pretty slow, put it in neutral, and by the time I coast down the hill to 13th Street, the wind is so strong it's *whipping* around my face, bringing *tears* to my eyes, no kidding, that's how fast I go, my split rim tires spinning like a top. I take a right and another right, and then I'm at my apartment. It's so quiet I can hear my heart above the whir of my four motors. It's a neighbors-are-gone kind of quiet, so I turn Etta up loud enough to drown out the sound of me hyperventilating. I lean forward, my head between my knees, my cells all grabbing the knife in their chest. Some tough cookie.

I skip the next week of class, and then it's Thanksgiving break. Tyrone picks me up and we go up to Louisville. We play war with the volume control. On, off, louder, softer, slap, slap. He's a stinker, but I finally let him win. We all gain fifteen pounds, but it's nice being home. When Tyrone and I get ready to leave, Mom gets all misty and shoos us out the door with a bag of leftovers and a couple of twenties each. When I go back to class, LG's absent, so it's almost three weeks before I see her again, and by then my heart is hardened, impenetrable, a rock. It's the end of the semester and Ms. Terrell invites us all to her house.

When I arrive, PP and 3 Ts are sucking up, asking Ms. Terrell about her house. I curl my lip and roll over to the food table. Might as well load up while I'm here.

"How long did it take you to renovate?" PP asks.

"Over a year. You see that fireplace mantle? That alone took me all summer, since it had about eight coats of paint covering what you can see is really beautiful woodwork."

"Wow. You did an amazing job."

"The best part is that there's a cave under my bedroom."

"Wow. Really? A cave?"

"Would you like to see it?"

"Wow. That would be really great."

Everyone follows Ms. Terrell as she leads them outside. PP hangs back and in a sugary voice, says, "Shamari, would you like me to push you so you can take a look, too?"

"I'll pass. I've seen caves before."

"Have you?" She looks down at the chair then leans in and says, "Don't worry, *she's* not going to be here." She gives her hair a shake as she walks to the doorway, then turns on her heal and looks back over her shoulder. "And if she does come, you probably shouldn't count on her being too interested in you, now that you helped her with her quote unquote *power* point."

She leaves me in the wake of her wave of mean, feeling like a serious loser.

Then I get mad. What am I doing sitting alone in the middle of someone's living room while everyone else is doing the tourist thing? "Wow," I say, then, "fuck that," and push myself down the hallway and out the door. I can hear them around the side of the house, so I turn to the left and get in line, behind guess who just arrived. LG doesn't hear me pull up, she's so busy talking to Ms. Terrell, something about her horse being sick. Or maybe she's pretending I'm not there. I inch forward, as the others, in groups of three, climb down some cement steps, through a dark opening, which makes the voice in my head go, Hmm. They emerge after a few seconds, and since there's no room to wait on the sidewalk, they all tromp back inside. When it's just Ms. Terrell, Molly, and me, she looks back.

"Hey there. Long time no see."

I grunt. Ms. Terrell frowns. "How are we going to do this, Shamari?"

"I don't need to go down there. I can see well enough from here."

"I know how," Molly says, and in her bossy way, without asking my permission, she swoops me up and carries me down the steps and into the darkness. I have no choice but to put my arm around her shoulder and try not to appreciate the way she turns this way and that so my legs don't bump the wall and the way she hunches down so our heads don't bash the ceiling.

"Are you all right?" Ms. Terrell calls.

Molly answers. "We're fine, we'll be out in a sec."

"All right then, I guess I'll go on in. I've seen it before." She laughs.

A lantern propped on a ledge casts a dim light. "I'll set you down here." She lowers me to a stone bench along the wall, then plops down beside me.

"You didn't have to do that, you know," I say, in my pretty chilly voice.

"I wanted to."

"Why?"

"I've missed you."

"Hmm. I'd think if someone missed someone they'd give some-one a call." I pinch my lips over the whine coming out.

She's quiet, then heaves a great big sigh.

"You're right. Call me a bitch."

"I can do that. I guess in the company you're keeping that's to be expected."

"You mean Presley?" I can feel her looking at me, though I'm staring straight ahead at a rock wall. A series of bolts has been attached to the wall, as if there'd once been shelves, for a root cellar maybe. I start to suggest this interesting historical tidbit, but she interrupts me.

"The night I stayed with you, Presley and I had been going out for about six months."

You could have knocked me over with a very soft breath.

"But she was just experimenting. Another straight chick seeing what it's like."

"Maybe you like experimenting, too."

"Maybe I like you."

Tears start to my eyes and I have to clamp down hard to drive them back.

"And then my horse got sick and almost died. That's why I wasn't in class last week. I've had her fourteen years. I slept in her stall, so I could call the vet the first sign of it getting worse.

"But you know who I was thinking about while I curled up in the straw and watched the moon pass by the stall window?"

"Look, I'm trying to stay mad at you."

"I thought about that night, just kept going over what it felt like to have your sweet little body next to mine. I thought about when we were at the computer putting our presentation together, and you kept saying 'Let's try this' and how your fingers flew over the keyboard, making things happen. I thought about your mouth and the way your lips stretch over your teeth when you smile. I kept feeling my hands going—"

"Stop it, Molly."

"I don't want to stop. I don't like fake. I don't do fake. Or, I guess I should say, I can't stand myself when I do fake."

"Well, you know what Etta would say."

"What would Etta say?" she whispers in my ear.

I turn toward her and take a millisecond to study the shadows of her face. "'When you see me again I hope that you have been the kind of person you really are now.'"

She whispers into my mouth. "We're leaving together after this is over, right? I have something to show you. No point in asking what because I'm not telling."

the kind of person you really are now

It's not a problem getting into a car, usually. I lower the arm on the left side of my chair and heave-ho. It helps to have someone to pack up the chair, but I could do it if I wanted to. Molly's got a truck, so it's higher up than a car. She helps me in and then loads the chair.

We drive in silence. Even though it's December, my window's cracked, it's that warm.

"I've never been out this way. Do you drive this every day?"

"Just about. Western's horses are over there, and my mom lives just a ways further. We grew up out in the country, but it's only about twenty minutes from campus."

We turn off Nashville Road and head up a long winding hill, then down and up another hill and down a long drive that ends in a yard, half gravel and half grass, between their house and a barn, with fields reaching in all directions, and beyond, the woods. A wave of country hits me as she sets the parking brake.

"It smells good," I tell her, but she's already out of the car and setting my chair up next to my door. She wheels me into the barn, where I'm hit with another wave of country, this time animal and leather and something else, like molasses.

"Be right back," she calls and leaves me in the middle the barn. Sticking their heads out of their bedrooms, three horses watch me with obvious interest.

"Hello," I say, and one of them makes a funny noise and shakes its head. They stomp their feet and flick their ears. The black one lets go with a big whinny.

I feel like sharing, so I say, "I feel that way too, especially at the end of a long day."

Molly emerges with a contraption that looks a lot like a saddle.

"What are you going to do with that?"

"I'm going to throw it over Hasbeen's back and tighten the girth. He likes to inflate himself so I have to put it on then mess around with his food till he lets it out, then tighten it again. I don't want you rolling off!"

"I know you heard me mention that I don't like horses."

"That's why you need to go for a ride with someone who does. But first, introductions."

She leads me to the first one. "This here is Babe, my best friend," she says. Babe has caves above her eyes, which are soft and shy looking. I think maybe old horses aren't so bad. Molly puts her forehead against Babe's nose and gives her a kiss, then leads me to the next horse, a big black thing who looks like he could get annoyed very easily. "This is Iago, my sister's horse. They're inseparable. That's why we took out the wall between their stalls, so they could sleep together. . . . And this is Hasbeen."

She opens the rest of his door and leads out a big brown horse with a tail that flicks this way and that like he's nervous. He shakes his head and whistles through his nose.

"I don't think he's in the mood."

"I'm going to put you on the saddle and I'm going to sit behind you, okay? This here is the pommel, and you can hold onto it. I'll have the reins. I won't let you fall. Promise."

It seems unfriendly to refuse, so I try looking unhappy, but she only laughs.

"Shamari, welcome to my world."

She straps on the saddle then leads the horse over to an old wagon-looking thing and comes back for me. Handing me a jacket off a peg and slipping on one herself, she says, "It's liable to cool off," then helps me up to the wagon. She hauls a bale of hay from one end over to the edge of the wagon and pats it, so I know to pull myself up. She takes Hasbeen on a stroll around the barn and monkeys with his belt, then brings him back. The horse is so close I can see his eyelashes. Molly jumps onto the horse behind the saddle, then grabs my right leg and I slide off the bale of hay. Suddenly I'm sitting on something big as a fallen tree, only it's moving. Molly takes the reins and pulls them across the horse's neck, which he understands to mean go left. If this beast minds at the touch of a piece of leather, maybe it will be okay.

We head into a big field, and Big Head's ears move forward and back. He begins to trot, or whatever it is that makes your butt slap the saddle.

"Slow up, Hasbeen, we got time."

"Is Hasbeen really has been?"

The sun tilts toward the tree line in front of us.

"You can lean back, if you want. You don't need to be so tense. See what a gentle boy he is?"

I try leaning back a little and she tightens her arms around me, tucking her chin over my shoulder. We don't say more, just jiggle with the horse, and gradually my stomach relaxes. I lean back a little more and she lets go of the reins with one hand and reaches into my jacket and under my shirt. The back of my head hits her shoulder as she presses her lips into my neck.

We head into a valley, where we can see across a series of fields, rolling ever downwards, to a melting sun that seems to be winking at me.

"I have to ask you something," I say, "And it kind of helps that I can't see you." She lowers her hand and lets it rest on the saddle between my legs.

"Do you feel sorry for me?"

There's a moment of silence, then her lips brush the back of my head again.

"You mean like pity?" When I nod she goes on, "Shamari, I'm more likely to feel sorry for animals than people. Everyone's got problems, and yours don't seem worse than anyone else's. You think that's why I'm interested in you?"

It didn't seem so outlandish a few hours ago.

"You're the one who gets to drive around in a cool chair."

When I don't acknowledge her joke, she says, "I guess when you're different you have to wonder what people's motives are. Like me and Presley. The last time we were together she told me that I could never be like a guy, but since she wasn't seeing anybody it was nice to have someone safe to mess around with. Something different from the same-old."

"And you think that's the same as sleeping with a crippled black girl? You think I'm safe?"

She pulls the horse to a halt. "Turn around."

"What do you mean?"

"I mean, turn around here." I twist toward her and she grasps me around the waist and leans all the way back on the horse, so that I end up on top of her, completely unseated. When she sits back up, she has somehow turned me around so my legs are over hers and I sit on the saddle facing her.

"How did you do that?" I start to ask, but her tongue takes my words and loses them. I can feel the horse through her, shifting his feet, tilting his hips.

"Can you lean back just a little?" She asks so nice I give it a try, putting my hands on the saddle behind me. She unbuttons my shirt, and when she notices my bra latches in the front, she says, "What have we here?" In the cool air, the cells of my skin rush with arms in the air to the warmth of her mouth. My eyes follow the horse's long neck past the mane with its coarse black hair falling to one side, up to his ears, where the sun, hooked, is now melting into the trees. At least if I fall off this horse my mom won't have to worry I died happy.

Her voice is husky and low. "We'd better head back before it gets dark."

I lean back on that pommel thing while she lifts my right leg to the side so I can turn, then we lift my left leg right over the horse's neck. Once I'm good and locked into place, Molly turns Hasbeen toward the barn. She makes a clucking sound. "Hang on!"

The wind rushes past my face and I gulp the evening air.

"Lean forward. Let go with your left hand and reach down. Feel his shoulder."

I shake my head and she says it again, "Lean forward. Let go."

She leans with me and holds my wrist as I open my hand against his rippling shoulder. It's wide and warm and I can feel the shock of the ground coming up through his leg, then air as he bends his leg through space, then ground again as it comes down. I think about this horse's legs, skinny to the knee then a big ball like a burl, then more skinny leg till it widens and meets the shoulder and the big engine of its body. Ground. Air. Muscle. Wind. It's a body that says *run,* I think, and then I'm saying it, too, *run, Hasbeen, run.*

Achers Pond

You are so impatient! Yesterday, you kept snatching at a strand of hair that had escaped your barrette, and while I helped you get Daniel settled in the kitchen, your mouth was all tucked in. At least Daniel was too sick to notice. Maybe that was it. But you didn't act mad at Daniel. You're always nice as pie to Daniel, so maybe you were mad at Daddy for being gone so much, working on the *damn* Kentucky Dam Village, over near Paducah. Oh, why pretend, I know who you can't stand to look at anymore.

I tried to get you to listen to the composition I'm writing for school, but you kept saying, "Not now, Sarah," or "I've got to get these sheets washed for Daniel." I stamped my foot. That didn't work, nor did *non-stop chatter,* which you said would drive you to distraction. That's why yesterday, while you were cooking and Daniel was tucked in the rocking chair where he could watch what was going on, I read it to him instead.

"Daniel, listen to my composition and tell me what you think. It's called, 'Yesterday, Today, and Tomorrow.' Here's how it starts.

"'My name is Sarah Lynn Collins. I was born in 1925, on a cold, snowy day in February, in my home outside of Bowling Green, Kentucky, which is on the Barren River, and which was the Kentucky capitol of the Confederacy for a brief while. Last summer, with the Great Depression on its last legs, as my daddy says, thanks to our great President Franklin Delano Roosevelt and his New Deal, Daddy and my uncles built our house, and my brother Daniel helped. My mother and I mostly cooked and did the regular chores. I had fun running through the rooms and playing house with Daniel. It was fun to stand in our back door and look at the distant woods and the fields and the pond, which glitters on bright days like a big sparkling quarter.'"

Daniel laughed, "Oh I like that part." I glanced to see what you thought, but your back was turned as you kneaded pie dough at the butcher block, so I went on.

"'My mother is Louisa Lynn Collins, and my daddy is John Everett Collins, and they were both educated at Berea College, which is where I will go some day. They tell me that when I am sixteen (which is only two years away), we will take a trip there and stay at Boone Tavern. I could go to Western Kentucky State Teachers College, but I would like to leave Bowling Green. My daddy is an engineer for the TVA and he's helping to build the Kentucky Dam Village, where a town called Gilbertsville is going to be flooded. My mama was an English teacher until Daniel got too sick, and then she quit. I am in high school and I make straight As. My cursive is almost perfect; except when I'm in a hurry, I cross my Ts way too high. I also like to give the Ys and Gs a big loop, like they're going to snag something from the line below. I am going to be an artist someday.'

"Should I take that part about cursive out? Hmm?"

"Probably." You finally lifted your head, though you still didn't want to look at me. "It doesn't have anything to do with what your title says it's about."

I set the pages down and drew a line through the words. "Too bad, that's my favorite part."

The next bit would probably be better left unsaid, since it told how Daniel was born with his cord wrapped around his neck, which explained why he is not as smart as me, because of lack of oxygen. "'He came down with polio,'" is what it said, "'and later spent time up at the Crippled Children's Hospital in Louisville, where a bone specialist named Dr. Barnett Owen started the free hospital for kids. Not only is Daniel frail, but he gets infections too easy and has a tendency toward pneumonia. I used to think that after piling everything up on Daniel, God made it so that when I came along my parents would have no more worries.'"

Instead of saying all that out loud, I just read, "The rest of my family is Daniel, and he is my best friend even though he is ten years older. That's all I have so far."

Daniel looked disappointed.

"I've got to add a lot more about you, of course."

"That will make it better," he said.

That was yesterday. This morning, you finally gave in to Daniel's request to get out of the house, even though the doctor said to stay in bed for a week. Every day this week I have gone to his room so he could listen to me do homework, but after he had all he could stand of πr2, he'd say, "Does it look like it's clearing any, Sarrey?"

I'd set my books down and go to the window. "Not yet, Daniel. The rain has stopped, and the clouds are nimbostratus." Ever since my teacher gave the A+ on my science paper on cloud formations (with illustrations), I've been keeping the terms fresh by using them in everyday conversation, though I doubt you noticed.

"How about today? What kind of clouds today?"

"There's blue now and the clouds are cumulus, which means puffy, like cotton."

"My favorite is nimbus," Daniel said, but he was referring to the word not the cloud.

Then this morning, the sun dried out the yard, so you said we could go to Achers Pond.

"I want to put my hand in the water. I want sunshine," he said as I packed the picnic, which included a blueberry pie that got blue juice on everything else. "Never mind," you said, your mouth like a door closing. You hitched up Golden to the chore wagon, and I piled blankets and pillows against the bags of grain that were under the seat so Daniel would have a soft place to sit. Then I got in and we rode the short ways down the hill to the pond. Our heads jiggled against the grain bags, and I pretended my head was going to fall off. "My innards are going to be scrambled eggs," I said, and he said, "Mine are, too."

While you let Golden loose to graze, I made a place for him in the green canoe, which is wide enough for us to lie down side by side, with you in the one seat for paddling. We like to feel the water underneath our shoulder blades, only this time you had me get on the seat.

"Oh, it's tippy," he said, when I got in. "You'll fall in and drown me!" Sometimes the line between us disappears. When I was little and we slept in the same room, he used to say, "Take a deep breath so I can yawn, and then you'll fall asleep."

You pretended not to be worried. "Don't be a silly goose," you said. "See how Sarah Lynn has hold of the sides? Now just lift this leg . . . there you go . . . now your right. Now grab hold of the sides and sit down. Slow and easy does it."

He was perspiring, and what little color had returned to his cheeks during the wagon ride had drained again. He swayed, then sank to his knees.

"It went dark for a minute. I ain't used to being up."

You waded in and pushed us off, saying, "It's a good thing we took our shoes off. Look at this mud! I'm going to have to let my feet dangle over the edge and wash off." Water just rolled off the thick glob of clay, so you had to use your fingers to pull it off.

Rowing with my back to the other shore, I looked back at the house on the top of the hill. The downstairs windows winked, and the leaves of the oak tree fluttered, like butterflies, away and back, away and back. For some reason, the sun wasn't reflecting against the loft window where my bedroom is. It was flat like a blind eye. If you drew a pencil line straight down, you'd come to Golden, who glanced at us then returned to snatching up the new grass.

It was too pretty a day to be mad. "I'll take you on a little sightseeing tour first," I announced, "then we'll paddle out to that island you see yonder, where we'll be the guests of the mighty warlord, who is really only a fish with big dreams."

I circled the pond slowly, past the row of willow trees, past the spring that you always said is what persuaded you and Daddy to buy the Achers' place. On the far side, Daddy and Daniel's dock looks like it did the day they stopped when Daniel got too sick to work. I rowed around a second time, and we pretended we were seeing wild animals along the way. Even though I could tell your heart wasn't in it, you said, "Is that a gazelle I see over there?"

"I don't see nothin'," Daniel said, then, "Unless you be talkin' about that scrawny thing next to the hippopalthomas?" You smiled, probably thinking about his piggy bank hippo that sits on his bureau and is named Thomas. But I know more than you do about Daniel's names for things. Like the steps going up to the loft: Big One, Little Toe, Johnny Step, Stop It Step, Tony, and Tony Again.

The sky was the prettiest soft blue and came down on a breeze that lifted the hair off my forehead. I used to look out at that same blue in February and think for a second that winter was gone, but when I stepped outside the sky had tricked me, the blue cold as ice.

I couldn't get used to a fine color like blue being anything but the color of warm. Green, now there was a color for icy storms and frozen streams. According to my art appreciation book, blue is a cool color, like green, but to me, blue, like yellow, means warmth, soft breezes, bare skin. Green, like red: an inner chill, time to hide. And purple, the color of shame.

We had reached the raft, so I grabbed hold and tied us up. You were so excited when Uncle Joe and some of his friends built it while my daddy was out of town. When Daddy heard how they got it in, he laughed. It floated on eight metal drums that Uncle Joe got at the depot downtown, and it took six men to move it into the water. "I'da built it in the pond or put it on a platform and just tilted it in. But I guess you boys needed a bigger challenge." It had been a challenge, all right, getting the raft anchored in the center. But finally they got it right, heaving over four big rocks tied to the raft with ropes just long enough to reach the bottom. Daniel and I swam every day for the rest of the summer. The only bad part was walking in, because of the mud. I don't even like to touch the bottom of a bar of soap after it's been sitting in its dish overnight. Daniel, however, would have been satisfied squishing in it all day.

I climbed onto the raft and stood. You pulled out our lunch and Daniel leaned over the edge of the canoe, watching reflections of the raft wobble the green-brown water, as he stirred with his fingertips. It felt peaceful up there, and you didn't seem cross anymore as you made a table over your and Daniel's laps. I sat on the edge of the raft, my toes pushing the rope that held the canoe. I lay back and closed my eyes.

A low boom, like hunger from the stomach of a giant, made the pond shiver and sent a wave racing toward the shore. The raft dipped so the corner hit the water, then bounced back. I flipped onto my stomach and looked right into Daniel's eyes, where there's a little brown dot in the middle of his blue. The raft vibrated against my legs and I heard a distant waterfall, but it was muffled, so I wasn't sure. Was it the wind? The pond looked ripply with white caps. Where the shore should have been, a thick slab of shiny brown was smeared, as if by a large thumb.

"Get off that raft, Sarah Lynn!"

I jumped into the canoe and untied the rope, as the raft and canoe began to turn. In moments we were facing the half-finished dock. With its long naked legs reaching into the mud, it looked like an old lady lifting her skirt and stepping daintily out of the muck.

I grabbed the oars and pushed one of them against the raft, then drove them into the water and pulled until I was standing up.

"What's happening? What's happening?" Daniel cried.

"I think it's a sinkhole busted through," you told him, trying to make your voice calm.

His hands beat the air around his face. "Oh, no!" He was looking at me.

I pulled harder on the oars and curled my toes around one of the ribs of the canoe. You started to get up, but Daniel grabbed your arm. "It's tippy! It's tippy!" he hollered, and you sat back down.

"Sarah will get us out of here. It will be fine."

It seemed that the canoe had finally turned away from the raft, but no matter how hard I drove the paddles into the water, it kept pivoting back. Something wanted the canoe, along with the raft and the rest of the pond. I let the paddles fall into the canoe as it knocked back into the raft. The remains of the shore raced toward us, gobbling fish as it came.

We had turned so we faced the house again, back where we had started. Underneath the raft, the barrels grated against the edge of the hole and the raft came to a stop. Water streamed between the barrels, along with fish, several turtles, and an old shoe.

"Look at the fishes!" Daniel cried. "One, two, three . . . Sandy, Mandy, Candy, Randy . . . seven, eight, nine. Bye-bye Horace! Bye-bye Norris! Be sure to write." He counted twenty fish, then lay back, exhausted.

Against the sound of water draining, silence rang, as if something had been peeled back, then gradually the sounds returned, or had they ever gone? Birds gathered in distant trees, a fly buzzed past my nose, the canoe—or the raft, or both—creaked, and the sun grew hot.

"What are we going to do?" I asked when you kept looking over your shoulder.

"I'm not sure. I'd like to get us out of here. How about if I try walking in and get us some help? See how far you can stick your paddle into the mud."

Holding on to the handle, I pressed it in, and the pond swallowed the blade until I couldn't push any further.

"I think I can make it."

"What you gonter do? Where you gonter go?" Daniel grabbed your arm. "You can't walk in that. It'll pull you down and if you fall you can't get up."

This made sense to me. I knew I wasn't about to put my feet in there. "There could be snapping turtles under the mud," I said, as a way of backing up Daniel.

You settled back onto the seat. "I just don't think we can wait here doing nothing."

"Isn't Daddy coming home this afternoon?"

"Supposed to."

I could see you were worried. The excitement was exactly what the doctor said was hard on him, and though Daniel had hold of your hand in both of his, I could see his grip was gone.

We waited, watching the fish grow sluggish and the flies swirl in. I kept track of two turtles making their way out, but they were so slow that I lost sight of them twice. You helped me spot them. We had our picnic. Daniel fell in and out of sleep. I got sleepy, too, and was halfway dreaming when Daniel asked you to tell about the time when I was born. He loved to hear this story, especially in front of company.

"It was a cold and wet February when Sarah Lynn was born. You were ten years old then, and your daddy had gone up to see what was going on with his cousin Floyd, who was stuck in a cave."

"He died that way, didn't he?"

"Yes, but he was still alive when your father went up. Sarah Lynn wasn't supposed to come for another two or three weeks, and Floyd was the biggest news in the country. Not that they were close, mind you. They only met once, but your dad and just about every other man and boy had to go to see for themselves."

"I wouldn't like to be named Floyd, would you?"

The sun was warm and the smell of the pond bottom made us thirsty. I plugged my nose and tried breathing through my mouth. You had passed me a pillow and now I leaned against the side of the canoe and closed my eyes.

Your voice droned on, circling and going deeper, inside my head: *Daniel is putting on his winter coat and boots, because he and Mama are alone and I am starting my long journey into the world. Even though he tires easily and it is more than a mile to the nearest neighbor, he is the only one who can go. The snow comes down in big pancakes that catch on his eyelashes and make him laugh. He knows the way even in a hard snow.*

A shadow crosses the sky and I can't see as well. The snow comes down thicker and begins to swirl. I press on, though my feet have gotten heavier. I lean into the snow that has laid a white blanket over everything, taking fence posts and trees, all the landmarks. I am in a cloud. A dark spot is the only thing to follow. My legs are shaking when I get to the house and bang on the door. I must have collapsed because when I wake up I am inside and Mrs. Bellows is holding a cup of coffee to my lips.

"What happened then?" Daniel was saying.

"You told them your baby sister was coming and wouldn't someone go help your mother. Then Mrs. Bellows started moving in a hurry, and Mr. Bellows went outside to go to the midwife, but his truck wouldn't start. So, he had to saddle a horse to go get her."

"What happened then?"

"After Mrs. Bellows warmed you up at the fire and got some things together, she saddled their other horse and the two of you came on back to the house."

You smoothed Daniel's hair away from his face. "You were my brave boy that day. You saved your sister's life. And maybe mine."

He looked at me, but I pretended I was sleeping.

I wish I didn't have a brother who is dying. It was more fun when he could carry me on his shoulders, or we could swim together, or go downtown and visit with the children who lived there. I heard Mrs. Bellows tell you that we were fortunate to have time to get used to losing him, as she did not have that opportunity when her own son died in the first war. It was crazy to talk about getting used to no Daniel when Daniel was right beside us, every day of the week.

"Daniel is your guardian angel," you said once. "Not everyone has a guardian angel, and most don't get them while their angel's still here on earth."

Lately when we go to visit them, Mrs. Bellows just wants to reminisce. Maybe that's why you never want to leave the house for long anymore and Daddy doesn't want to come back. And this has to be why you are Unhappy. He didn't need to stay away so long, you said when he came home for the first time in over a month, and that was just two weeks ago. What if Daniel needed him? Daddy talked in his low rumbling voice, persuading you like he always does. "Daniel's not going anywhere this month."

When it came to recollecting, Daniel was even worse than Mrs. Bellows. Lately he was downright pushy. Just yesterday, after I finished doing my homework, he said, "Now that yer all done there, let's remember when. You tell about the time we painted fire hydrants." I set my books aside and flopped on my stomach next to him where we both could stare out the window, our chins resting on our hands. I fixed my eyes where he was looking, and in that square of light in a darkening room, we looked all the way back to that summer of 1935.

"I was ten and you were twenty, when we got to be part of real history. Part of the New Deal, it was called the National Youth Administration, and all across Kentucky boys like you were working on projects, making $10 a month. You and four other boys got the job of painting 250 fire hydrants in downtown Bowling Green. You all stayed in town at someone's house—"

Daniel's eyes brightened. "That was Edgar, and you got to stay with Uncle Joe."

"Yes, he had a couple of rooms in a boarding house on Main Street. Mama and Daddy were gone to Louisville, where our Grandma was ailing.

"Every morning we got up early and while Uncle Joe went to work, I played in the streets with other girls from downtown, and in the afternoon you came and got me and we painted fire hydrants. Yellow or red. One day, you left me alone with the very last hydrant, and you and the others took the supplies back. The boy in charge wanted to go meet some girls behind the—"

"That was George and he had two girlfriends that didn't know about each other."

"So anyway, George told me just to throw out the last two paint cans and brushes when I was finished. I got an idea to paint this one red and yellow, and so I planned where each color would go and ended up with a little man who had a red hat on and yellow trousers, a red belt, a yellow shirt, and a red vest. When the boys came back they said I would get in trouble, but you said, 'It's beautiful,' and asked me what his name would be."

"And then Conroy said, 'His name is Stupid, Stupid.'"

"That's right. So, I picked up my red paintbrush and flung paint at him. That got the other boys laughing, till Conroy came after me and tried to punch me. You maybe couldn't run fast but you could punch like the dickens. You took the air right out of that Dumb Cluck.

"Now here's the best part. I got up on your shoulders with a red paintbrush in one hand and a yellow in the other and we marched all the way back to Uncle Joe's, singing 'John Jacob Jingle Heimer Smith' at the top of our voices and me waving my paintbrushes like flags."

"And those other kids was marching behind us. What a racket."

"Did you have a good nap? Looks like Golden is back. I didn't realize he was gone, but here he is again. Sometimes I think the dumb animals are blessed."

"I need to use the commode."

"So do I. Let's do, while Daniel's sleeping."

"Do what?"

"Just hang your fanny over the edge of the canoe. No one's going to see."

Squatting on the edge of the canoe, I twisted around and tried to see into the darkness between the barrels. Peeing made a loud sound, so I hurried, pushing it out faster. Even though I didn't have anything to dry off with, I didn't like having my bottom next to the dark space, so I pulled my pants back on and then got on my knees and leaned into the opening. The cool air with its wet rock smell rose above the heavier smell of mud. It smelled like a tomb just opened, and in that smell, I could feel a great hunger. Maybe for the light of day.

"Sarah Lynn?" I didn't like how your voice had gone soft, like you were trying to be careful. "Can we talk about what happened? I mean, about your uncle . . ."

"But Daniel—"

"He's not going to hear anything. Look at him. Sound asleep. . . . I don't want to upset you again. Do you care if we talk about it?"

I had been looking at Golden, who was way above us now that we were at the bottom of the pond. I glanced your way as a cloud crossed over. "I'd rather not."

"Okay, but I'm going to ask you again. Maybe when we get out of here."

I lay back again and pretended to be asleep. Up until a couple of months ago, Uncle Joe was my daddy's favorite little brother. He was always lending a hand, and years ago he helped out by watching me when Daniel had to go to the Kosair Crippled Children's Hospital in Louisville. The last time Daddy looked at me was that night and then ever since, away. I was the one who made our daddy stay gone so long.

I turned toward the cool, rocky air again. What good would telling do? No! I didn't want you to know the way time disappeared, until something woke me up with a little pinch, and there I was, in school, next to Daniel, at the dinner table. It said, *This is who you are.* Tell that to you? No!

In my mind, I reached into the space where the cool air met the rising stink of mud and fanned it toward myself. Was there a way to tell and to not make you mad? What part could I leave out without you pulling it out of me? I kept my head resting on the side of the canoe so you would think I was sleeping and wouldn't guess I was finally telling you, just in my head.

I was four years old when I stayed with Uncle Joe so you and Daddy could take Daniel to Louisville. I was there for three nights; it was always three nights. Every day, Uncle Joe found something for us to do, and while he was at work, Mrs. Barclay took care of me. Every night we went for walks and he read to me and said how everything was going to be fine. I stood at the window to see if you were coming. Before bedtime, he let me play in his bathtub with the big lion's feet. There were three little boats, a breath mint tin, a red pipe that blew bubbles, and a little ball painted like the world. He filled the tub with soapsuds and got in then lifted me in and laughed while I played.

"I've got a tugboat," he said, "and if you pull on it, it will go 'toot toot,' say it with me."

"Toooooot, toooot," went the tugboat, until it sank. The red tugboat turned a darker red and sometimes even purple. It sank into the waves.

"You're my special girl. I know you're going to make your mommy and daddy very proud of you. Tomorrow they're coming home, and you can tell them what a good time you had with Uncle Joe and how you didn't miss them at all."

I don't like bathtubs with their tall white sides.

Then I was six; I remember because Daniel was excited to be sixteen at last, and Uncle Joe took us to the fireworks outside of town. Daniel wanted to go get some waffles, so Uncle Joe gave him a dime. We had a blanket spread out and a picnic. I wanted to go with Daniel, but Uncle Joe said stay. He reached under my skirt, his fingers in front and his thumb pushing into my bottom.

"Let's straighten your dress out first," he said, "And stay away from those nasty boys."

I caught up with Daniel, and he said, "Isn't Uncle Joe nice to let us get treats?" I nodded and thought how I mustn't let any boys get near me. But I couldn't eat the waffle. That night when I went to sleep in my own bed, I could feel his fingers digging. I can feel them today.

I was ten when I started spending the night with him again, because Daniel had a relapse and you had to take him back to Louisville. "Mind Uncle Joe and do what he says," you told me before you left. *This would make you feel guilty, so if you look sad, I can leave it out.* And Daddy slipped me a quarter and said to use it wisely. Sometimes Uncle Joe took me to a movie.

He used to tuck me in and curl up behind. He said he knew a way I could give him pleasure. "Squeeze your legs together," he would say, "and hold this handkerchief." Sometimes he had me lie down on my side with my stomach pressed to his back while he reached across me with his arm, then my hand went faster, slower, harder, softer, whatever he said. If I took my hand away, he put it back and held his hand over mine until my fingers were hot and sore.

We went to a square dance. He took me shopping for a new dress that afternoon. He liked the green one with bright red apples on it. I was twelve, and two boys my own age danced with me, and also Mr. Barclay, who said my apples looked good enough to eat as he breathed alcohol into my face. Then Uncle Joe left the pretty woman he was with and danced with me. We were laughing and sweating and walked home holding hands. He let me take my bath first, then he used the same water for himself. In bed he whispered, "You know, I can take you on a magic carpet ride."

He rubbed my back so slow and easy that I started dreaming, then he rolled me on my back and pulled off my panties.

"Let me show you what those pretty women know. You're prettier than they are, and you might as well know what they know."

Something was breaking, as I rocked against his hand. He moaned and hugged me till the throbbing died down. When he fell asleep, I slipped out of bed and left the house. I understood now that there was nothing he couldn't do to me. I walked all the way to Fountain Square and sat on the bench listening to the water crying, until I fell asleep. A policeman took me back to Mrs. Barclay's just before dawn. When Uncle Joe woke up, I was on the floor, in my own bedding.

My dream begins with me flying through a dark cloud and landing in a foreign country. I stand in a kitchen that I don't recognize. I am cutting stew meat at the butcher block and suddenly his hand is reaching under my arm. I grab his wrist with my left hand and hold it on the butcher block. I am so strong that he cannot pull away. Then I lift the butcher knife high in the air and bring it down, chopping off all four of his fingers. The blood shoots out everywhere, the window blows open, and a cold wind rushes through the room.

Remember how you used to complain that I must be staying up late and reading because I was always tired during the day, stumbling and dropping things? *Maybe I shouldn't say this either. It will make you feel guilty.*

And the last time you already know about. You and Daddy and Daniel were all in the house, and Uncle Joe and I were feeding the horse and cow and moving bales of hay around. *Why did you leave him alone with me?* He lifted my dress from behind and pushed me against a railing, so it was digging into my stomach. He was groaning and then choking.

I must have screamed, because you and Daddy came running in. Daniel had the reins around his neck, and the bridle was clanking around his knees. Uncle Joe's face was twisted and his eyes were starting to bug out. Daddy said what the hell is going on here and separated them. Uncle Joe kept saying, "I didn't hurt her! Get your idiot son away from me." And Daniel left and came back with the rifle and pointed it at Uncle Joe's head.

"You was raping Sarrey."

Uncle Joe was still coughing and rubbing his throat.

"No, I wasn't, John, I swear, was I, Sarah. She's still a virgin, John, I swear."

I reached my hand down and felt a wet spot on the front of my dress. I tried to run out, but Daddy grabbed me.

"Did he touch you, Sarah Lynn?" His voice was getting louder and rougher.

"He was hurting her! He was hurting her! I saw! I saw!"

"Take her inside, Louisa. Find out what's going on. Daniel, give me that rifle 'fore someone gets hurt."

You led me up to my room, but I was so sick that Daniel saw us that way, like a couple of dogs, that I would not let you pull my hands from my face. I did let you undo my dress and I let you look at my underwear.

I knew you were mad at me and that Daddy would be so embarrassed that you would make me leave the house. You would say that if that's the way I was with Uncle Joe, I could just go live with him. We could get married and carry on all we wanted. I knew that was impossible because it would be incest, but I couldn't imagine where else you would send me, except maybe a home for bad girls or a convent. By the way you said, "You stay here till I say you can come out," I knew that you would not want to know me anymore.

I could hear yelling outside and then silence, voices under my window, more silence. He was still saying how I was a virgin, and I heard you hiss, "And you think that's the only thing you can steal from a little girl?"

Uncle Joe's truck started up and drove off. Then Daniel came in. He didn't climb up to see me, he just dragged himself into his room. I leaned into the hole in the floor and listened. I could hear the springs of his bed when he flopped down on it. Then only the sound of the grandfather clock chiming the hour. I thought of how I loved Uncle Joe and how he loved me. I wouldn't ever see him again. Then I thought of how Uncle Joe waited till I was nearly asleep before starting in. Sometimes it seemed like a dream, where I was floating on a cloud that turned to a carpet that flew with a rush. It got dark outside and still you did not come for me, though Daniel had left the house again. I was crying into the bedspread when you and Daddy both climbed up to the loft.

"Your father and I want to talk to you, Sarah Lynn."

You sat down on either side of me, and each took a hand from my lap. You patted yours, but Daddy just put his hand over mine and squeezed it. I remember thinking how different your hands were and how much I loved each one.

"Can you tell us what happened?"

I shook my head.

"Is this the first time he's made you do that?"

I shook my head no. *It never occurred to you that I never told him to stop.*

"How many times?" When I didn't answer, you said, "More than twice?" I nodded. "More than five times?" I nodded again. I tried to catch a glimpse of Daddy's face, but he had turned away and let loose of my hand.

Then he spoke. "Did he ever put his . . . his . . . ?"

I shook my head no.

"Did he hurt you in other ways?" he asked.

"I don't know! Are you going to send me away?"

"Good heavens, child, we're not sending you away!"

"It's that son of a bitch we sent away."

You didn't ask any more questions and we avoided his name from then on. But Daddy looked at me different after that and didn't hug me the same way. You started acting impatient and looked like you were mad. Daniel used up all his energy strangling Uncle Joe, and got pale and slept more, until he got pneumonia, which is why he wasn't allowed out of bed, until today, when you broke the rule and brought us all out here to the pond.

I looked at you and saw you watching me. "Can I whisper it?" You lifted your arm from under Daniel's head and crawled over. I placed my lips against your honey hair and was about to whisper the beginning when I heard our names, "Louisa! Daniel! Sarah Lynn!"

For a frozen moment, the voice seemed to be saying, *Don't tell.*

Then you jumped up, and I heard myself say, "It's Daddy!" and Daniel sat up and looked around, bewildered.

"What in sam hell happened here? You pull the plug?"

We all started yelling at the same time, trying to tell what had happened. Daddy started to come across, then thought better of it and went back to the barn for rope. When he came back, he flung it like a lasso, but each time, the end fell short. So, he tied one end to Golden then waded in, about a dozen steps, and flung it again, and this time I caught it as it slithered over the canoe. He hollered to Golden and they pulled us to solid ground.

He helped Daniel up, then lifted him, and started toward the house. "We had us an adventure, Dad, and Sarrey took us to a lot of foreign lands, and we almost fell in, but she saved us. She was very brave."

I couldn't hear his answer. Daniel's thin legs dangled and his left arm rested on our daddy's shoulders, as they made their way up the path toward the house.

That night I dreamed that a giant stood outside our house, pulling dark green clouds stuffed with thunder and lightning from all the skies of the world, balling up the nimbostratus, snagging the cirrus wisps against treetops, and bundling them together and hurtling them as hard as he could. The house shook and the windowpanes rattled, but the cloudbursts couldn't break through. The giant lowered his eye to my back window and looked in. It was Uncle Joe's eye, big and bloodshot and darting around. His fingers wiggled at my other window, and the house started to shake. Downstairs, he was using a battering ram. The door swung open.

I sat up and looked around. Moonlight poured through the window, and leaning forward. I could see that the sky was clear and full of stars. A terrible loneliness came over me. I didn't like it up here at the top of the house anymore, where I could not tell if you all were downstairs or had left. I got out of bed and lay on my stomach at the opening to the loft, listening. Nothing but the grandfather clock. I climbed down and stopped in Daniel's doorway. His room, too, was filled with moonlight. I went around the bed and climbed in beside him.

"Yer cold, Sarrey. Whatsa matter, you couldn't sleep?"

It was strange looking at each other in the night when it was so bright from the moon. His eyes were dark and glittering in his pale face.

"Mama and Daddy love you best. You're always good and I turned out bad."

"I ain't so good as all that and you ain't so bad."

"Name one thing you've done bad recently."

"Well, that ain't so hard. I stole some tobacco from our father. I used to do that a lot and sneak down to Achers Pond to smoke."

"You shouldn't do that. Mama says your cough is worse when you smoke. That's why she took your cigarettes away."

"I know it. I just can't help myself. What bad thing you done? It ain't yer fault the pond drained out. You didn't pull no plug."

"I know," I whispered. "What do you think they'll do with it now?"

"I heard Dad say they was going to find a way to plug it and let it fill up again."

"I didn't know you could do that."

"He said it happens all the time around here."

I pulled my hand free from his and lifted a strand of hair from his temple. "What am I going to do without you, Daniel?"

"I ain't goin' nowheres, Sarrey, not really. I know what yer talkin' about, but you ain't got to worry. When I go to heaven, I'm still going to watch out for you." He patted me on the cheek, then pulled his arm back under his blanket.

"What you scared of?" he asked.

"Giants."

He chuckled. "Well, there ain't no giants, Sarrey, except in storybooks."

We were quiet for a while and I thought he had drifted back to sleep. I tucked my toes further under his knees.

"When I get scared, I talk to God and then I get a peaceful feeling. Do you talk to God, Sarrey?"

"God is too far away and too busy."

"Why he's right here in this room. Sitting on my dresser over yonder. He likes to sit inside Thomas and watch us from there. I want you to have Thomas, Sarrey."

"I don't want you to."

"I talk to Mama about it sometimes when yer in school. She said that we're still gonter talk to each other and see each other, but it will be in a new way. I get awful weak you know, it seems like I'm made of water. One of these days there ain't goin' to be nothin' left to sit up with."

Daniel's eyes flickered shut and his lips parted as his breathing evened out. How easily he went to sleep. I could feel the moon shining on my face, and yet his was lit up, too. I was glad he knew how I loved him. Maybe Mrs. Bellows was right, but I didn't see how knowing could be easier than not, or how the heaviness behind my eyes could be anything but an eternal sinking of my heart.

Something unknown and yet known was happening in the next room. It seemed as if I could see Daddy staring at the ceiling. Earlier, I heard you crying how you were sure that he had been unfaithful. Before tonight this would have made him mad, but tonight he could see how things were for you. The past two months he has avoided home, but today, seeing us stranded in the middle of the pond, all three of us waving to him . . . that had knocked something loose. And seeing your face when you cried out that he didn't love you anymore had sent that loosened thing floating up so that now it is tapping against the back of his eyes.

Something known and unknown, in the next room, the way he loves you and how, even when you're asleep, your body gives at his touch, as though your skin is talking to him. He runs his hand along the warm soft length of you and speaks into your ear. "Are you asleep, Louisa?" You turn toward him, slipping your arm over his side.

Outside, the moon fills the night sky with a brightness that slides over the land, catching at animals' eyes and dipping the butterfly leaves in silver. Achers Pond glimmers, the mud drying in places while in others the water still shines in shallow pools. The bodies of fish lie about, and at the pond's edge, a raccoon searches for a firm place to enter. The raft looks the same as it did this afternoon, caught at an angle in the center of the pond, the cool air that slips between the barrels shimmering, a ghostly light released into the world.

Who Do You Love?

From her eyes, sparks ignite the dust motes, which churn in the trail of her passing. She leaves without saying goodbye, though the closing door speaks loudly enough. Silence bears down, ringing and pulsing, heartbeat of the empty house.

Beside the fireplace the giant geode squats, an egg-shaped gnome, head bent over his exposed belly, as though stunned at the exposure of those brilliant crystals inside. There, over the years, daughters lowered fannies, crying, "Ouch! Ouch!" as they leapt up, the backs of their legs red-marked, indentations they read with their fingers, bending slightly and reaching back, mock pain. She carried it home from a trip out west, seat-belted into the back seat, next to their first-born, who rested her hand protectively on its shoulder.

He can imagine Gnome coming to life, reaching inside itself, and offering up the crystals, like organs. "Take these as well," using her voice. It's a miserable thing that the one who might understand leaves in anger and frustration, enabling the house to raise the volume of its incessant grumbling. Windows and mirrors are inhabited by a mottled face, the grandfather clock mutters. The mirror over the mantel reflects the top of the entryway to the kitchen, where hangs a long rectangular photograph of the white gypsum formations of Carlsbad Cavern. A house so marked by her (save his already cooling first book of poetry now stacked in leaning boxes in the corner) that even in her absence, the house uses her to snag him.

The last full night's sleep, when was it, three months ago?

She's not the only one who can leave. Let the door slam on the rocketing silence. With no human presence does the house relax its malicious hold on things? No way to know. Leave it to the next imposter. The car, a neutral bullet, speeds to its destination. At work, the desk is a wall of papers and books. In the space between the two sets of drawers, his knees find refuge and hands fold themselves over the deserted armory of his lap.

Already, there's knocking at the door. Students want their papers, they're still exultant from last week's reenactment of the Parable of the Cave. A reporter from the student newspaper called it, "Professor Probes Parable." Quoted him: "I took to heart Plato's injunction that education is the art of turning around, not the art of putting the capacity for knowledge into the body—it's already there." Summarized him: students played the roles of the enslaved and the image-makers. After a period of time, the first prisoner/student escaped his bonds, saw the mechanics behind the images thrown on the back wall, and made his way into the light, which was blinding, at least at first. Then he (or she) circled back and became one of the image-makers. One by one, the others followed suit, so by the end, all twenty students had played all the parts.

A theoretically endless circle. So much effort, thinking it through in the early morning hours, finding the equipment, coordinating all the pieces.

They liked the idea (this was better than sitting in class), made jokes about bondage and pornographic shadows on the wall. They divided the black theatre lab into three sections: at the very back twelve of them faced the wall chained to each other with a real chain, their hands and necks fettered; in the center, the other eight took turns prancing in front of a strobe-lit fire, sending grotesque images of themselves against the wall, grunting, chanting, roaring occasionally, moving their arms in sinewy lines, holding up cut-outs of horse and pig heads, a pitchfork, a large phallic hammer. Behind them black curtains separated the world of images from the world of true knowledge. As they stumbled out of the darkness, one by one, they covered their eyes, but of course, there was nothing there, the whole point being that truth, though not "out there" in the *X-Files* sense, is not just inside either. Only the capacity.

They performed spectacularly, seemed to pull closer (another quote). "Great class, great professor," they said, talking about it in the hallways. Now in a stack somewhere on the desk, unread, their parables wait. Due next week: an essay about the experience, what it has to do with their real lives. Did this ever make pedagogical sense? Now it seems grandiose, buttressed by the certainty that he was both a great poet and a great teacher. Thoughts of congratulations and fawning admiration made it impossible to sleep. Now he was unable to face colleagues with their red leering jokes about probing. Flat-featured as the cut-outs the students had held up in front of the dancing strobe. What if it wasn't admiration but disdain that pulled their faces so ghoulishly?

And worst of all, the last two weeks bored with her—the truth? Too good for her. Now lucky if she even recognizes the wreckage. She doesn't like the parable—no wonder, caves are her life. "Why does the cave have to be the place of greatest ignorance?" she wants to know. Last week, when they were talking about the idea, her friend, the feminist philosopher, wanted to know, "Why this hierarchy of knowledge, with the senses way down at the bottom? Knowledge ripped from the body is no knowledge at all, only arrogance." They laughed, superior in their dismissal. Thoughts of slapping her, fucking the other one. *No wonder you hate me.*

Students knock, wait, some try the handle, but eventually they all give up. The lights are off, no one's there. The window shade allows a thin outline of light in the shape of a rectangle. A great mushroom of sadness pushes against his heart. Bile rises. So horny, rocking against a pillow on the floor, imagining first one student then another, each crying out with pleasure-pain, their breasts bouncing and tongues wagging as they crash down on his burning thorn.

In the halls, classes change, feet march past, loud burst of laughter right outside the door, a secret told, "Meet me after class." A departmental meeting starting in fifteen minutes. Impossible. In her office the phone rings and rings and eventually transfers to the office secretary, who parrots, "Hello? Hello? No one's there," before hanging up for the third time.

Come get me, my life. I'm in pieces on the floor.

They'd fallen in love at a Doors concert—so many years ago, before their lives merged and the girls arrived—she'd joined the group in Lexington, riding together in a van to Pennsylvania. "Who Do You Love?" she laughed, dancing in the crowded aisle. He grabbed her arm and kissed her to "Love Her Madly," shouting to be heard, "want to meet her daddy." Over the years, touching her shoulder, her face, the top of her head, answering, "this one," the question, "what do you love," unstated, their inside joke reaching back to the night they fell in love, he at first sight, she later. Which of these do you love, she'd ask, looking down and smiling up, knowing what she'd hear: "This one, no, this one, no . . . " Now voices wag from the books, *this one, this one.* Touching spines, trying to still them only stretches the words, so they become *thisss-ion-sion-sion,* not real words, sibilant, then *mission—this one, mission.* He's just tired, hearing things. The college chimes mark the passing of another hour. Across the hall, a class erupts in laughter. The sounds in Cherry Hall layer like hands of children trying to determine who will go first, each moving a hand from the bottom of the pile and slapping it on top, endlessly climbing. Footsteps from the floor above, fainter ones from the third floor, and on the roof the flapping wings of pigeons, sighs of professors who have died. The aging furnace ticks beneath the window, marking the seconds. Let it blow. But it only sighs as it shuts off.

Silence rushes in like water. He imagines the pain as a toxic mushroom in his belly that rises, squeezes past the larynx, pushes his lips open. He can imagine it bubbling out, now that it's outside the body, a jellyfish of unnamed need pulsing as it rises above him then floats down, tentacles tickling. Frantic probing at the belt buckle, as though it wants back in. Only sleep might put it to rest, but sleep is a line that can't be crossed.

The need to urinate becomes urgent, but even at 2:00, the halls are a glut of eyes, hands that tug, personalities that pull against skin, snagging the thin layer. Does urine kill plants? One way to find out.

3:30, another round of footsteps, the last till night classes. Someone knocks, her silhouette leaning in, listening. A taller shadow comes up behind, covers hers. "Is he there?" She must be shaking her head no. "Figures, that asshole never meets his office hours. Let's leave a nasty message on his board." The female voice objects, then giggles.

5:00, leaving the post beside the door, his eyes having traced the perimeter of the room 350 times: line, line, circle, ray, angle,

angle, dot, ray, line, line. Fifty-seven lines, thousands of rays, dots marking the ceiling panels like clusters of stars in remote galaxies. The mission: to note each one and assign it a place in infinity. A spear of light daggers across the floor, nothing to stop it from piercing the body, pinning it to the wall. No longer a solid, he has gone glutinous. Extraterrestrial, fitting to the human shape because, well, that's how to move through a hostile environment without calling attention to the alien within.

6:55. With pants lowered, his exposed thigh hooks the blade. Thin red lines begin to etch her name, *Meredith.* The phone stops the blade on the fourth letter.

"David? David?" Let her taste silence. "Are you there? I've already checked home." More silence. "I know you're there, I can hear the chimes. We were supposed to meet a half hour ago." A long sigh. "I'm sorry I walked out on you this morning. I'm not mad anymore, just hurt. I know you're having a hard time. We knew you couldn't keep up the pace, you'd have to come down to earth sometime. What are you doing there? David? I'm coming over now. Sweetheart? Let's not break each other's hearts, David."

The door is unlocked now. Boo Radley waits in the corner. She will find this body and fold it in her arms like a thing well loved. Pointless to hope for an end, pointless to long for a new beginning. He can see her walking up the hill, bent forward, determined, eyes down, then up, glancing toward the window, noting the drawn shade. Can feel her enter the building, bursting through the door in a feast of light and fresh air. The sense of her precedes even the sound of her feet as she approaches the door. The quiet turning of the knob, so as not to startle, but then a pause as she clears her throat. Her voice, beloved above all else, rises, "Darling?" and underneath, "I'm scared."

She is all surrender, meeting his urgency with whispers, snapping the lock too. *Who do you love?* Her eyes hover on his thigh—is she looking at, no, it's the bloody name, *Mere,* that makes her shudder so. She steps closer, her hands rise then disappear as she grasps his neck, her arms say, *this is an embrace.*

Better not to look.

"Come with me, David," she says softly, as she turns toward the door. "My car is just outside. They've got a room for you. It will be okay. I love you. You just need to rest. Later we can talk." The voices mutter in exasperation, ruffling the pages of the books on the shelves, diving in to wait among their comrades. *Get back! Get back!* Holding her hand makes the sparking nerves shift tracks, the way a truck, careening out of control takes the runaway ramp at the side of the expressway and burrows into the deep-layered, speed-swallowing gravel.

Her hair is soft beneath clumsy poet fingers. She pauses, looks back, her eyes under water. "What, my love? What did you say?"

Lost River

She didn't need to tell him how wrong she'd been or apologize for never calling. She needn't explain how she'd been busy, first going to school, then working at the hospital. He didn't want her to call out of guilt or pity or even nostalgia. In fact, she didn't need to say anything. The call would come, and though silence would meet his "hello?" it wouldn't be the silence of an empty line, but rather of Cecily holding the mouthpiece away from her mouth so he wouldn't hear her breathing. He'd say, "If you want me to come over now, just hang up."

Five years ago, roughly if not surprisingly, they'd gone down in flames. The actual burning of the house had been her fault and leaving her on the lawn after he'd pulled her out unconscious—that had been his fault. She'd told him it was over. Sleeping with his cousin Josh had been her way of proving it. Since the house belonged to Josh and it was his lab that blew, neither of them had been charged. At Josh's funeral, the casket was closed. The other users came to pay their respects, making connections in the parking lot on their way out. Derek sat in the back row, a human mummy from the waist up. No one approached him.

Returning to his parents' home in Morgantown, he'd stayed in the back room for ten weeks. Shattered was the word his mother used. His face oozed where he'd torn the bandages away, then scabbed and finally scarred, leaving smooth tracks around his eyes and mouth. He spent the next month listening to their rock collection and emerging only to eat and mow the lawn. "Guess I'll go back to school," he told them one morning. He'd returned to Western, where he spent the next two years lifting his 1.9, notch by notch. He burrowed into schoolwork the way an addict hunkers down with a pipe, *this is all that matters.* He worked in the

Education Office and ended up with four top-notch references, including the dean's, which got him a job in town right after graduation. For his junior and senior years, he pulled a 4.0, which one of his professors encouraged him to put on his resume. "I see it often enough," he said, "But not so dramatically. It's like there's a dividing line between your sophomore and junior year."

Derek just nodded. There'd been a line all right. A lot of lines.

It wasn't as if he thought about Cecily every day, except recently, oddly, making him long to hear her voice. At first, missing her had been a cement block that he'd carried—in his stomach, across his shoulders, between his legs, in his throat. By sheer will he had levered her away, gritting his teeth through over-work. It was three years since she'd told him never to call again and two years since that brief glimpse in Kroger's, where she bent over the scanner checking her purchases, and he passed with his cart, turning once, twice, three times to look.

Recently, he felt launched from his apartment, like being shot from a canon, to the streets of downtown Bowling Green. And whenever he left home, rocketing into the streets, he found himself counting. He counted how many steps it took to get from one corner to the next, how many passersby, how many birds on a wire, making math problems as one flew off, two returned, five left. Leaning against a telephone pole, he told himself that passersby assumed he was waiting for his ride. They glanced at him, nodded, lifted fingers from the steering wheel.

One night he threw his dirty clothes into a basket and headed for Wishy Washy. As he stepped inside the same long-limbed girl he'd seen at the library, at Spencer's, even waiting at the stoplight, cast him a surprised look and left. Another night, taking the long way home to his apartment, he'd seen her emerge from Micki's on Main. It was a rainy night, and a streetlight caught her friends in a yellow smear. In the middle she was blue, rising, a trick of the watery light. They stood beneath the overhang, laughing, then ran to her car. He'd followed her to her apartment on 11th Street. She paused before she entered and looked over her shoulder at him, as he passed. Now he stepped back outside the laundromat and lit a cigarette. She had pulled out, one taillight winking. He went to the vending machines and ate a candy bar, then another. He didn't stop until he ran out of money, then folded his clothes and went home.

That night he'd drunk more than usual, sipping bourbon and flipping back and forth, *Gunsmoke/The Daily Show, Gunsmoke/Insomnia.* When he stood up too quickly, he fell over the coffee table and cut his shin along a newly splintered edge. He sat on the edge of the bathtub and watched the drops of blood track through the hairs on his leg, then rush over the anklebone and drip to the porcelain.

Like this, they had sat on the edge of the bathtub, laughing at how water slopped over the edge when they slid in together. She'd looped her arms around his neck and pulled him to her, sliding her tongue into his mouth.

His third graders were beside themselves as they lined up behind the guide, two rows of blond, brown, black, and red heads.

"Mr. Thompson, is our school named after Lost River Cave?"

He gave her the look. "Now, Lucy, we talked about that yesterday."

He knuckled her cornrows and she grinned up at him, her smile taking up most of the lower half of her face, parenthetical with two dimples.

"Mr. Thompson?" Her small hand tugged at his elbow. "Are you going to wear your life jacket?"

"It's only four feet deep. The water would only come up to here."

Satisfied, she loosened her grip. "Will you sit by me?"

No one else was clamoring for his attention, so he nodded.

The path to the cave entrance led them past a blue hole, Ripley's shortest river, running only 400 feet to the cave entrance. Once believed to be over 400 feet deep, the pool was actually only ten feet deep, linked with the underground river, where a current once deposited things miles away.

The guide's voice got low and he looked around, as if he didn't want anyone else to hear. "In a similar incident three soldiers went swimming, one didn't come back, and his two friends, one by one, dove in to see what they could grab hold of. They were never seen again."

Forty round eyes met his.

"Is that how come they call it the Lost River, 'cause of people getting lost?"

The guide turned a page in his mental notes. "Late in the 18th century, some people found sawdust that was dumped into the water here in a pond about three miles away. That's when they realized there had to be an underground river connecting the ponds all along."

Lucy peered over the railing, into the greenish blue water.

"It don't look anything special," she said. "Looks like my grandma's pond."

"I don't care what it looks like. You wouldn't see me dive in after they didn't come up!"

This was met with a chorus of "Me neither" and "That's straight" and "I would . . . for a million dollars."

Getting them into the life jackets took almost twenty minutes of checking, wandering, taking off, putting back on, and finally loading into the boat.

Almost immediately, they had to duck their heads as the boat floated beneath a slab of lowered ceiling. Derek could see a series of cracks, inches deep, cut through the surface. They looked like they were about to give. Lucy's elbow gouged into his thigh as she leaned forward. "Tell me when it's over," she said and buried her head in her hands. The ceiling lowered silently, but personally, toward him, and he pressed his face between his knees and told himself to breathe. As he tilted his head to see how much longer before they cleared the ceiling, Lucy's puffy braid brush against his mouth. A clutch of panic rose in his throat. He pushed her until she lifted her elbow and her head dipped away. He gulped as a rush of air met his lungs. Then the boat slid out from under the slab, and they entered a large cavern, the ceiling rising sixty feet above. Lights set up along the walls showed different formations and tiny streams of water that fed the underground river. They all sat up, a collective sigh shimmering across the water to the cave walls and back. He felt sick.

A voice, under his left arm: "It smells funny, don't you think?"

"Smells like a outhouse to me."

The guide pointed out a drapery formation, as the children's comments bounced off the walls. They had opinions about everything: the temperature of the water, cool, not cold, the scummy green and yellow mineral formations dripping off the walls. How scary it was, and dark.

"Keep your voices down. Let's hear what he's saying," Derek said, his own voice like someone else's as soon as it crossed his lips.

"Thank you. Now, kids, I don't want you to worry, but if a drop of water falls on you and it's cold, that's called a cave kiss. If it's warm, it's called a bat kiss."

"Oooh, gross. Are there really bats in here?"

"Yes, and if you follow my flashlight, you'll see one right now."

"Is he going to suck our blood?"

"That's only in the movies. Bats are shy creatures. They help control the insect population."

"I'd like to take some of them bats to my house to eat lady bugs."

"Do you have a lot of lady bugs?" the guide asked.

"They infestate our house all the time, expecially in the spring."

Lucy raised her voice, "Mr. Thompson says they ain't lady bugs. Don't you, Mr. Thompson? They're Mexican bean beetles. Ladybugs are red, and these are yellow, and they have exactly 16 black dots on their back."

A wave of déjà vu washed over him—Cecily sitting beside him on the hard metal seat, her arm reaching behind him and her fingers playing his ribs. "Isn't that right, Derek?" she was saying, trying to get him to talk. He could smell her hair, a hint of orange in the damp cave air.

In truth, that last night she'd been so high she didn't know who she was, kept saying, "What's my name? I can't remember," then laughed and chanted "fuck me, whoever I am," moving from Derek to Josh, back to Derek. At some point, she disappeared, probably passed out or wandering in the woods, then returned toward morning when everyone had finally crashed. Down in the basement, she stuffed Sudafed backings and empty containers of acetone, toluene, and Coleman fuel into a trash bag. Leaving a trail of lighter fluid, she had reached the top of the stairs. The explosion knocked her out of the basement and toppled her into the kitchen. Derek woke with burning lungs when he heard the scream of a cat cornered in the next room. He watched it leap through one flame into another. Fire slapped the doorway, and beyond, the kitchen careened away. He lurched forward, saw her unconscious, legs cockeyed and her head wedged between the floor and the bottom of the cabinet. The kitchen was already beginning to fold into the basement as he pulled her out. Once outside, he saw a shadow moving in the living room, where Josh had sealed himself, after doing loud things with Cecily that Derek had run from, ready to kill Josh or himself or Cecily.

He staggered to the window and threw a brick. It bounced off, then a small hole appeared and a crack. Sucked out by the sudden pull of air, smoke rushed to fill the window, swirling, as the window shattered, and Derek fell back. When he came to, his face felt on fire, and when he ran his fingers over his cheek, they came away with blood and a shard of glass. He put both hands to his face, felt the rough edges of a dozen pieces of glass, and realized he was seeing out of only one eye. Although the smoke had cleared from the window, in its place a row of orange flames had begun to dance. The room where Josh wavered had devoured him. Behind Derek, Cecily lay under the tree, her face flickering orange, and beyond, the sound of sirens poured over the hills. A voice—hers, his, no one's—urged him to the woods, *run, run.*

Back at school, Lucy skipped up to him, something clenched in her fist. He was standing next to the line of buses waiting to take the children home.

"Here you go, Mr. Thompson, I got this for you."

She opened her hand and turned a jagged piece of glittering mineral onto his outstretched palm. He thanked her and slipped it into his shirt pocket, then hurried to the back of the line to keep two boys from shoving their way into a fistfight. He clenched his teeth. "Now why do you two want to go and spoil a nice day, huh?" His voice, harsher than he'd intended, surprised them. "He started it," they both insisted but climbed meekly into the bus. He got them seated, one in back, one in the middle, and was moving to the front of the bus, when he heard Lucy's voice.

"I'm going to marry Mr. Thompson some day when I get old enough."

"How old do you have to be?" asked her seatmate.

"I'll be sixteen and he'll be twenty-five. That's how old he is,

I know, because I saw a birthday card on his desk, and it said 'Happy 25th Birthday.'"

"When you turn sixteen, he'll be forty-two or something. You can't just freeze him till you get old enough, Lucy. That's retarded."

She looked out the window, then turned back. "Then we'll move to Iran. Mr. Thompson says that they lowered the marriage age down to nine."

She saw him then and blushed so deeply that her brown skin took on a rosy glow across her cheekbones. He pretended not to notice as he jumped down and headed for the faculty parking lot.

Pulling onto Morgantown Road from the Natcher Parkway, he caught up with one of the buses as it turned on its flashers. He waited behind the red blinking lights and extended stop sign and looked around. It was a bright day, a stunning contrast to the darkness of the cave, where he had momentarily lost it. He pulled down the visor so he could see the skinny legs of three girls pile out. They ran across the road and raced up a long, paved driveway that led to a house, tucked behind a row of houses that sat closer to the road. They were older girls than his students, longer limbed, faster, louder (well, maybe not that). He saw the driver in the gray Mustang facing the bus in the next lane duck his head for a moment, then a fourth girl, moving slowly, stepped across the yellow line, her arms hugging a book to her chest. He watched as the Mustang leapt forward and flung her back toward the bus. By the time he reached them, the bus driver and the Mustang driver were at her side.

"Oh, sweet Jesus, I didn't see her." He was a skinny boy with stringy blond hair.

Derek knelt beside Lucy as he pulled his cell phone off his belt, his fingers fumbling with 9-1-1. She watched him, her eyes darting from him to the knees of the other two.

"Where's Mommy?"

He looked toward the house, where the three older girls had headed. Beyond them, the front door of their house flew open, and a large woman bolted down the steps. The girls looked at her, then back toward the bus. One of them ran toward her. The other two dropped their book bags and galloped back to the bus.

"She's coming, you just sit tight."

The kid in the Mustang danced from foot to foot and clutched his hands under his armpits. "Is she okay?" Derek felt a wave of pity for him, though the bus driver snarled, "She'd be a lot better if you hadn'a run into her."

Lucy tried to look past Derek, toward home. "Mommy," she cried, and it seemed that her voice had thinned.

When Mrs. Jackson knelt beside Lucy, Derek leaned back to give them room.

"I feel funny. But it don't hurt."

Lucy's mother looked around as though trying to decide which of the three men could answer the unspoken question in her face. "There's an ambulance on the way," Derek said. "I'll be glad to go with her, if you want, or if you need someone to stay with your other girls."

The three girls clustered behind their mother. One of them leaned over and began patting Lucy's head.

The boy wiped his eyes. Mrs. Jackson looked up at him.

"You do this to my child?"

"I don't know how it happened. I was looking at my phone and the car just jumped."

"You're in deep shit," the bus driver muttered. Behind him, the children had all piled to the side of the bus and were staring out the windows. One boy called out, "It's that guy's fault in the gray car," and Derek held his finger up to his lips.

Mrs. Jackson turned back to Lucy and gently felt along her legs. "I don't think these are broke. Can you squeeze my hand, Lucy?" she ordered. Lucy shrank under her bulk.

"What?" she seemed not to understand the question. She struggled with her tongue, then said, "I swam to the deep end, where the bats live, Ma. And the ceiling was falling but Mr. Thompson held it up."

"Where'd the car hit her?" She looked up at the boy.

"Her back," he said.

"Well, then, we won't try to move you, sugar. Those EMS folks will do that. You cold or anything?" Lucy looked at her wide-eyed, not answering.

"I've got a blanket in my trunk," the boy said. When he returned, he knelt down and handed it to the mother.

Lucy's skin seemed ashen. She stared at Derek and he smiled, but her expression didn't change. Her eyes had thickened, then they rolled back and her legs started to shake.

"Oh, baby, what you go and do that for? Lucy! Lucy!"

Mrs. Jackson lowered her body over her, warming her or holding her still, Derek couldn't tell. He looked away as a police car came to a stop beside them, then the ambulance.

He sat in the only extra chair, next to Mrs. Jackson.

Lucy's color had returned, though she lay unmoving, her thin brown arms resting on top of the white sheets and her face covered with a mask. Tubes reached from under the flowered hospital gown.

Mrs. Jackson kept her eyes on Lucy, as though she was speaking to her. "They saw something in the x-rays. Did it seem like she got hit hard enough to break her pelvis?"

"I really don't know. It happened so fast."

"Do you suppose that boy's foot slipped off the brake when he was distracted and hit the gas pedal? That ever happen to you?"

"I rolled into another car once, sitting at a stop light. I was taking off my sweatshirt."

"Well, when I put on the brakes they stay on." She paused for a minute, then tapped his arm with the back of her hand. "Sometimes it feels like all I do is ride those brakes."

She stood and stretched her back. "I work in this hospital," she said. "Up on the sixth floor, psychiatric. I have been so lucky. This is the first time any of my children has had to go to the emergency room. I been dreading the day, but you don't wake up every day and think, this is the day something bad is going to happen."

"You'd be scared all the time."

"I wake up every morning and get my four girls ready for school. And I just trust the Lord to watch over them. They look like stair steps when you stand them next to each other. One every two years for eight years. Lucy's my baby."

"I like Lucy."

"Well, she likes you, too. It's Mr. Thompson said this, Mr. Thompson said that. Truth be told, I was getting a little tired of you."

"I think she wants to marry me."

She laughed. "Now that sounds like Lucille. It surely does."

Tears seeped from her eyes. "Mr. Thompson—"

"Derek."

"Derek, Lucy's Daddy left at Christmas, and it's been . . . rough on her."

"You think that's why—?"

"That's why she don't pay attention. I bet she was planning her next visit, before that car hit her. Excuse me, Mr. Thompson, while I get aholt of myself."

A nurse appeared at the doorway, saw Mrs. Jackson with a Kleenex and made her voice gentle. "We're going to move her up to IC now, Mrs. Jackson. Sir."

They followed the nurse and Lucy into the elevator and then into the IC unit, to one of the last rooms. "I like this," Mrs. Jackson said. "It will be quieter for her back here." Then she leaned toward Derek and whispered, "Less trouble for her to get into when she's up and around."

An hour passed and they spoke only in reaction to changes in the sound of the hospital machinery or the appearance of a nurse. The tick of the clock seemed louder when he looked up and saw that Mrs. Jackson had been watching him.

"You don't have to stay any longer. You can check back any time."

"I'll stay a while yet."

She nodded and they went back to sitting in silence. Twice more, a nurse came by and took Lucy's vitals. He yawned, suddenly so tired he could barely keep his eyes open—the smells, the dull hum in the walls, voices from the hallway, disembodied laughter from the nurses' station—together, a narcotic.

After the fire, he'd gone to another room, on another floor, where he'd spent a week. During that time his face had been worked on three times. Although he'd intended to run into the woods and then away, he wound up on the same county road that the police took as they led the ambulance away from the burning house. He overheard them in the ER, standing outside his room. They were telling the nurse how they found him.

"He looked like Freddy Kruger coming toward us, walking down the middle of the road. We pulled over and he was talking crazy. I waved the ambulance down and Bennie there took one look at him and put him in the back with the girl."

The nurse spoke: "We're pulling the shards we can see out. He's been real still, just stares at the ceiling. If you push down on a piece he just clenches his jaw."

He felt a tear escape his eye and roll down his cheek.

"You all right, child?"

He nodded and sat up straighter. "Bad memories."

"You been here before?"

He reached up and touched a scar on his chin, his right cheekbone, his forehead, over his left eye.

"Did you walk into a glass door or something? My cousin did that. Wasn't as lucky as you though."

"No, it was more like a window coming out to meet me."

"You mean an explosion?"

He nodded and looked out the door toward the nurses' station. He felt his mouth drop. "And right out there is the person who almost died with me." He stood, knocking the chair back. He straightened it and stepped to the corner of the room. Mrs. Jackson leaned over so she could see into the hall.

"Well, if you're talking about the pretty brown-haired girl with those big round glasses, she's heading this way."

"Don't tell her I'm here."

He slipped into the bathroom where he could hear their voices through the door. "There's a new shift coming on and I'm one of the nurses. My name's Cecily. How's she doing?"

There was more, but he couldn't catch their words. Someone rapped at the door. "Derek? The coast is clear."

He pulled the chair back into the corner and sat down.

"Old girlfriend?"

"We got into a lot of trouble together, you can't imagine, and she doesn't want to have anything to do with me."

Lucy's hand moved and Derek pointed to her. Mrs. Jackson leaned over. "Hey there. How're you doing, baby?"

She opened her eyes and tried to smile. "My head hurts."

"Did you see Mr. Thompson here? He's been waiting the whole time. Come here, Mr. Thompson, and say hello." She stepped back to allow Derek room to stand next to the bed.

Lucy's face lit up momentarily when she saw him, then she turned away. "I thought you didn't like me no more. I made you embarrassed."

"Nah, nothing like that. I'm proud of you."

"And this lady here is one of your nurses. Her name is Miss Cecily, and she and Mr. Thompson are old friends, isn't that right?" she spoke directly to Cecily.

Cecily's eyes widened. She stepped back, the desire to flee written across her face.

"Mr. Thompson is my teacher," Lucy explained, her words drowsy. "Do you still have that gem I gave you, Mr. Thompson? You put it in your pocket up there."

He patted the pocket, felt the lump, and reached in.

"I thought maybe you could hang it in a window or something."

"That's a good idea. In fact, maybe we can do that right now. Is there a piece of string we could use?" Mrs. Jackson looked pointedly at Cecily.

"I think I can find some thread," she murmured.

Touching her hand as he took the thread from her sent a jolt through him. He wished he could see if she'd been affected, but he couldn't tear his eyes away from the sight of his fingers fumbling with the thread. He could feel her watching.

He laughed. "I can't get my fingers to work." He handed it to Mrs. Jackson. She had no problem getting a knot around the rock and a length for hanging it. She handed it back to him.

He tied it to the bottom of the raised shade. The rock hung down, catching the light.

They all turned to look at Lucy, but she was asleep.

"Well, then, I guess that's it for now." Cecily turned to go.

Mrs. Jackson reached for her hand. "I reckon you have a break sometime and wouldn't mind taking Mr. Thompson here down to the cafeteria for some coffee, now would you?"

She flushed, then nodded. "Sure, I can do that. If you're here that long," she added, glancing his way. "I wouldn't want to keep you waiting."

"Oh, he's not going anywhere. Are you, Mr. Thompson? He wants to make sure my Lucy's going to be okay."

"I don't have long," she said.

After they'd made their way in silence to the cafeteria, he said, "I didn't know you were working here." He had a piece of apple pie and a coffee on his tray. She had picked up a cup of yogurt.

"I wouldn't expect you to know much about me anymore."

"I'm surprised they hired someone with your record."

"We were teenagers, Derek. Look, if you have something to say, here's your chance. But I won't talk about what happened."

"Are you seeing anyone?" When she frowned and didn't answer, he asked, "Why are you so mad?"

She stabbed her spoon into the yogurt. Her voice quavered. "I'm not mad at you per se, I'm just not interested in reconnecting with old acquaintances from my miserable youth."

"Acquaintance. That's one word for it, I guess." He worked at his pie.

"Can I tell you something without you walking away or getting sore?" He watched her eyes for another sign of alarm.

"There's nothing you can say that can undo me."

"You're undoing me right now, and I don't care if you know that."

"Are you trying to tell me—? Why do you want to hang on to something that—" She closed her eyes, looking for the word, "—that old?"

"I'd be happy to erase you from my mind. I'd be happy to start over with someone who's smart and has a pretty face and a nice personality, but every time I try, I get bored."

"And that's my fault?"

He shoved the plate to the other end of the table, reached across the space, and pulled her hand toward him. She resisted but he held on.

"I haven't touched anything for five years, Cecily. Well, maybe alcohol, every so often. If I see someone from back then I turn and go the other way. I put myself through school and have a good job now, where these cute little kids look up to me. That little girl upstairs would rather sit by me than any of her classmates, and when she pulls on my arm to get my attention, it's usually something so cute that I—."

"That's very touching."

"I'd forgotten how cynical you are."

"I'm glad you pulled yourself together. No matter what you say, you were never that bad off. You always did see what you wanted to see. You look back at us and they start playing violins, or some shit. I look back at us and I feel a fist around my throat."

He felt like a balloon the day after the party, floating around the empty room, four feet above the floor and sinking. He looked down at the top of her head as he stood. He could see by the set of her jaw that she was listening. He made his voice quiet.

"I feel like I know something about you, Cecily—ever since that day I saw something inside you so beautiful I couldn't breathe. We screwed it up, but that doesn't have to define the future. You could try, couldn't you? Maybe see why I'm willing to stand here humiliating myself. Okay, then. I'm going back up to see Lucy now, and then I'm going home."

His heart pounded as he raced to the elevator. "You're my man of few words," she used to say. Hadn't he shown her another side, just now? Except for that line about seeing something beautiful, like he had super eyesight or something. She hated sayings like that. He seemed unable to resist them. Just don't do it, she used to say. You deserve a broken jaw today. I'm not worth it.

He greeted Mrs. Jackson with a small wave. "Has she woken up again?"

"Nah, but she's sleeping good. They're going to wheel in something for me to lie down on. You go on now, you been here for hours. I know a young, good-looking man like you has to have someone wondering where you are."

"Don't be too sure, Mrs. Jackson."

She stood as he approached to give her a hug. "You're a real gentleman, sure enough," she said, squeezing his back. Tears stood in her eyes. "I can see why my daughter thinks so highly of you."

The bar was long and dark, but in the warmth of spring, the ironwork tables had been moved out front, facing Fountain Square. He'd left a note on his apartment door, indicating where he was, just as he'd done every night since they talked. There had been no phone messages, no calls, and he'd stopped waiting. He sat at one of the tables under the canopy and watched people look for a parking spot, watched them approach, then go inside, watched them leave, some of them wavering as they stepped back to their cars, watched them drive away. The ice melted in his glass and the waitress stopped checking on him.

The blue-rising girl with the long hair drove by, and their eyes met. She parked. She stepped out of her car, tossed her hair as though she were doing a commercial for Pepsi-Cola. Her steps were long and purposeful. She glanced at him as she passed. Several minutes later she reemerged with a tall drink and gestured to the empty chair next to him. He pushed it back from the table with his foot and nodded at it.

"I've been seeing you around lately. You followed me the other day, didn't you?"

"I was curious."

"Are you a sicko?"

"Nope. Are you disappointed?"

"A little. What happened to your face?"

"I got jilted."

"That's happened to me before, too. But it didn't have that effect."

"You sure about that?" He reached over and drew a line in the air, as though tracing something. "Because I'm pretty sure I see a pale line right here, running down from the corner of your eye."

"You're kind of poetic. Are you a student?"

"I'm a teacher. Third-graders."

"I'm a grad student. I live around here. But I guess you know that already. I only drove because I've been running errands. I was thirsty."

They talked about the fountain, the best restaurants downtown, whether the city left the Christmas lights up all year. She seemed nervous and he surprised himself by tapping the knuckles of her hand. "You don't know what you're getting into, do you?"

"Not really. Do you?"

"You want to explore a little?" he gestured toward the fountain.

As they walked, her fingers touched his then curled away, her hand warm and dry, the bones long. Twice she bumped into him and apologized, saying she had a habit of listing whenever she walked next to someone. Her eyes caught the streetlights as they passed under them and she looked up. When they turned from Chestnut, his street, onto 11th, she stopped. "We got here fast."

I'll kiss her, he thought, but didn't. He could imagine her heart hammering against his chest, her breath against his mouth. He liked it that she was as tall as he was.

"I'm scared," she murmured. "I don't even know you."

"If you want, I'll leave. Give me your number and I'll call you next week."

"I'm scared you won't."

"Are you always this scared?"

"I'm never this scared."

He spoke into her ear, "How about if we walk back to 440 and get our cars? If you want, you can follow me. I live on Chestnut. I'll cook some linguini. We'll eat. It will be normal."

"I never liked normal, but it doesn't sound too bad, the way you describe it."

Aside from the intoxication he felt when her mouth opened to his—that was worth the price of admission—he thought, *wouldn't it be nice to place his words next to the words of someone else, someone in the flesh, who liked to be touched?* Someone who looked at him and saw more than ruin.

Movie Lines

A rain of dust settled over the blackened beams that lay in piles on the muddy ground. When they looked up, a feathery rain made them close their eyes and rub their noses. The collapse had deafened them, so they didn't hear Tyler say, "Houston, we have a problem." Or his mother's cry, "Where are you, Tyler?" Or Diana's shout. When the rumbling had faded, he heard his mother's voice, higher than usual, like the whine of trucks when the two of them drove down the other side of Kingdom Come Parkway into Letcher County. If there was a whine and then no whine it might mean the brakes had failed and you'd better get out of the way.

They reached out, squeezed an arm, a shoulder, found each other and crept deeper into the mine shaft. Tyler had wet himself and now the damp blue jeans rubbed his legs, so he walked like Festus on *Gunsmoke,* after he'd been riding all day, helping Matthew bring in some troublemakers.

"I think we'll be okay. The collapse was back by the entrance. My dad's going to kill me for bringing a stranger here and my own son."

Diana with the yellow hair and the orange streak said, "If anyone's to blame, it's me, Edna. It was stupid to leave my camera behind, after you were nice enough to show me around."

"Maybe there'll be some good shots along the way out of here."

"The danger's over, don't you think? Oh, shit. Ouch. Watch it, there's something sticking up. Can you shine that over here?"

"It's just a support beam. Look ahead, there's a bunch of them. Can you see?"

"I see dead people," Tyler said, watching as his mom played the light over a pile of what looked like bodies. They were stiff from almost a century lying there, and the miners had ignored them and eventually they got covered with old containers, empty lunch bags, dead batteries.

"Can we get around them?"

"Let's hold hands. Here, Tyler, you in the middle."

"You know, they do kind of look like bodies piled up here." Edna stopped and shone the light over the beams, catching a glint here and there, off a belt buckle and a pair of glasses.

The wet part was so cold he felt as if someone were rubbing an ice cube up and down his legs, and the jeans made a "thwick thwick" sound that he was surprised no one else could hear. He didn't have to think about running into something anymore. His mom kept sweeping the beam of the flashlight in front of them. It was all the same. Blackness, then cables threatening to snare them, then piles of dead people that were support beams. When they decided to take a break, Tyler sat next to his mom and put his mouth against one of the beams—how dirty could it be? —then changed his mind and lowered his head to her lap.

"How long do you think it's been?" Diana asked.

"Since we sat down?"

"No, since the crash."

"I can't tell anymore. Feels like six hours."

"What's Tyler doing? He's gotten so quiet."

"You asleep?" she pressed her hand against his shoulder.

"I feel awake . . . wide awake. I don't remember ever feelin' this awake."

Edna nudged Diana with her elbow. "That's from *Thelma and Louise.* He says it every night when I'm trying to get him to go to bed."

"I've never known anybody who talked only in movie lines. Tyler, what's your favorite movie?"

"You're not going to get an answer to that."

"Does he have favorite movies? Tyler, do you care if I ask?"

"You talkin' to me? You talkin' to me? Well, who the hell else are you talkin' to? You talkin' to me? Well, I'm the only one here."

"Which one is that?"

"*Taxi Driver.* With Robert DeNiro. His grandma has a collection. He watches them after school. He's got this memory where he can repeat anything someone said, even weeks later."

"I have a memory like a sieve, Tyler, so you're lucky you can remember things so well. It must make it easy to take tests."

"Trouble is he doesn't bother reading, just listens. I can't get him to read."

"Wait a sec. Did you hear that? It was sort of a whispering sound, like someone opened a door down the line and the breeze is just getting to us. Do you think they know we're here?"

"Mines make strange sounds."

Diana yelled but her voice just bounced down the long hall behind them and came slithering back, all wet. He wished she'd stop. She whispered, *"Something* has to make those sounds."

"True, but it doesn't need to be human. I wish my cell phone worked down here."

"Phone home."

"I guess even if your mom saw we'd left she wouldn't know where."

"She'd just roll over and go back to sleep. Figure, whatever. I wish we'd thought to bring some water. I ought to have my head examined."

"I could make love with a Classic Coke."

"I'm thinking lemonade. On the sour side, but cold. What about you, Tyler?"

"A martini. Shaken, not stirred."

"You wouldn't know a martini if it bit you. Come to think of it, I wouldn't either. I doubt Billy at the Scynus Parrott even knows how to make one. We'd better head on."

Every so often they had to step around a puddle of water. Squiggly wires dangled from the walls or lifted their necks from the floor in front of them like snakes. *It's alive!* Funny how snakes were just one long esophagus that became a stomach and then a butt. Maybe a little brain squeezed in there between the eyes. People weren't like snakes. Mom always said, "You have a big brain." Staring at the floor in front of them he felt the darkness closing in. Where did the pitch-black air stop and the hard rock surface of the walls and ceiling begin? In *Matrix*, Neo reached through a mirror and almost turned into liquid metal. He didn't want to believe what Trinity told him, *The answer is out there, Neo, and it's looking for you, and it will find you if you want it to.* He could feel the oxygen pressing tar down behind them, and he was sure he could hear that snake slithering toward them.

"You awake, Edna?"

"Yeah."

"Is Tyler?"

"No, he's sawing logs over here. Let's let him rest some then get the hell outta here. I just hope this vein has an opening at the other end. Be funny if we got there and found a cement wall where they closed it."

"I was thinking the same thing, but I didn't want to say it."

"Yeah, well someone's gotta say the ugly truths. I just hope I'm wrong. Always was a half-empty kinda girl."

"Do you care if I ask you something about Tyler?"

"You want to know why he only talks in movie lines, right? Don't know. When you think about it, there's just about everything a person can say in some movie or another. I've pointed that out to him. That he could say 'good morning' or 'thanks' or anything like that since people in the movies say pleasantries all the time. You can even say 'I love you, Mom,' and he just patted my shoulder. It's not the everyday things that bear repeating. For Tyler, anyway."

"How long has he been doing it?"

"Only about four months. I got mad at him at first, but he just patted me on the arm and said, 'Don't feel bad.' I don't know where he got that from. His teacher called a meeting and we talked to a counselor, but that butthole just made me mad. Said Tyler was acting out some problem in the family."

"It's not like he isn't communicating."

"Mostly he's just pointing out the humor in a situation, seems to me. When my dad got so tired of him not answering, he pulled off his belt, and Tyler hooked his thumbs in his pockets and said, 'Go ahead, make my day.' Dad started wailing on him, but he managed to roll away while I was yanking on Dad's arm. I told him if he ever touched Tyler again I'd kill him."

"What did your dad do?"

"He left, came back. Apologized. Took Tyler fishing. Dad's

pretty good with movies, too, so they just exchanged lines all day. At least that's how he put it."

"What about Tyler's dad?"

"Stupid fucking speedballer. Brain full of holes. Got busted for selling and accessory to the murder of one Paul Browning, who was running for sheriff of Harlan County, back in 2002. He'll be dead before he gets out. I took Tyler to see him a few times, but I didn't like how it made him. That was a year ago. We were walking back to the car and he looked over his shoulder and said, 'What a dump.' Some Bette Davis movie about evil. Mom said she thought he was asleep."

"He's a sweet kid. You can tell the way he watches and listens that he's thinking a lot."

"What about you? You got kids?"

"Not even close."

"So, how'd you end up on this project, here in eastern Kentucky?"

"It's my last summer with Appalshop. I've been working with them for the last three years, doing interviews for films about the region. It's what I want to do once I pass the bar—not interviews, but work in eastern Kentucky."

"Why? You gonna come here and save the ignorant hillbillies?"

"I don't see it that way."

"We get alotta that, you know, do-gooders and liberals coming in here to basically do alotta looking and talking before they move on. But not before they take a bunch of pictures."

"But I'm a Kentuckian, too, and I love the mountains. I love the people that I've met since I started working here. There's no denying the problems. I'd think you all would welcome any help you can get."

"Some help don't end up helping."

"As a lawyer, I think I could help."

"What is it they say about lawyers—? Ninety-eight percent give the rest a bad name?"

"Actually, I do know one movie quote about lawyers. What do you call 500 lawyers at the bottom of the ocean? A good start. *Philadelphia.*"

"So how are you going to save us?"

Their voices blurred into the blackness behind his eyelids. Or were his eyes open? He blinked again, trying to see something different in the behind and the front of his eyeballs. The only way you could tell someone was sleeping was if their eyelids were down. He wanted to find a way to sleep with his eyes open.

He needed to pee. The flashlight, which was sitting in front of them, cut a beam of hazy light into the swirling darkness. He reached for it.

"Everything okay, Tyler?"

"How would you feel if every time you had to take a piss you had to do a handstand?"

"*Reservoir Dogs.* That's another favorite."

He stopped a ways down the tunnelm, set the flashlight down, and unzipped his pants. His hands were cold and awkward, almost like they weren't really his. He pulled his thing out just in time, his hands so clumsy, and heard, then saw, the stream of piss hitting the flashlight and spattering the light. He made it go in and out of the darkness, and the sound went "shhh" then silence then "shhh" again. When he got back, he shone the light into Diana's face. Her yellow hair with the orange streak was covered with gray, and her face was smudged black, so her eyes looked up at him like they were floating in the darkness. He snapped the light off and handed it to his mother.

"Are you ready to walk, honey? I can't stand just lying around here anymore."

They stumbled as they stood to join him. He liked Diana, but he wished he hadn't shined the light in her eyes. Now he couldn't stop seeing her eyeballs. He reached for his mother's hand and she squeezed back.

They were talking again about the problems of eastern Kentucky. There was a good old boys network that took money out of the people's hands and spent it on big cars and vacations and houses with Jacuzzis. There were the Uncle Toms, selling out their own neighbors and getting in bed with coal barons like Massey. Oxy cotton turning people into monsters.

Get over here, you little shit. Put this balloon under your tongue, and don't bite it. Carry it around and let me see it. If I see any bite marks I'll kick your ass. Tyler slid it out on the tip of his tongue and let it drop into his father's cupped hand. That was the first time. The last time was when it fell to the floor and he covered it with his foot before the prison guard or his mother saw. Tyler winced when he leaned over to pick it up and his father's knee made his teeth crunch into his lip.

"You can tie your shoe later, kid."

He kept the balloon in his hand till he let it drop in the parking lot. *What a dump.*

When they got into the car, she handed him a Kleenex. He could feel her glancing over at him all the way home. "Don't let him get to you, Tyler, he's a shit.

"He didn't used to be that way, you know. You remember he used to pack you around everywhere? Used to read you the *Cumberland County News* and have you recite it to a roomful of his buddies. I didn't like him using you that way. But he was proud of you."

He'd squished the red-dotted Kleenex into the ashtray and turned on the radio. His teeth felt loose when he pinched them.

When they pulled into their driveway, she said, "That's the last time I take you there." They sat a while watching the snow fall through the back porch light.

He was thinking about springtime and the time he was waiting for his dad at his buddies' trailer. He sat on the step and rubbed the ears of their mangy old mutt, who always glued himself to Tyler's leg when he came over. The dirt was packed down hard where people parked their cars. A dandelion had taken root under the step, and now its yellow face poked out between his feet. He pulled it off the stem with a pop and sprinkled the tiny petals along Dog's back. Inside, they mixed up sizzurp. *Mountain Dew, phenergan, and codeine, that's the only way to sizz.* When they piled out, his dad pulled out a balloon and snapped his ear. "Do some Lil Wyte, Tyler," and Tyler stood up like the puppet he was, and went, "Scarecrow, scarecrow what's that you popping? A powerful pill they call Oxy-cotton. But it's so tiny, that it got you dragging. Haven't you heard big things come in small packages?" It was funny.

That was the time he drove the pickup the rest of the way home, sitting on the edge of the driver's seat, after his dad handed him the steering wheel and slid underneath him to the window and puked, then laughed and sat there bouncing and singing out the window.

He no longer dreamed about reaching into his mouth and pulling out a brown tooth so riddled with holes it crumbled into chalk when it hit daylight.

"Let's play a game. It'll help pass the time," Diana said.

"Well, I don't think *I Spy* is going to work."

"How about *Truth or Dare*? I'll go first. Give me a dare."

"Okay, I dare you to let out a belch so big that it echoes down this mine shaft."

"How'd you know I'm a champion belcher? Here goes."

Tyler held his breath while Diana with the blond hair and orange streak let loose a belch so loud his teeth vibrated. He and his mom both laughed.

"Not bad. So okay, my turn. I pick dare."

"I dare you to . . . Hmmm. I dare you to . . . cuss at someone as loud as you can. Only you can't use any cuss words."

They stopped walking when the light paused. "You're a piddling snotting two-timing butt-kissing poop-eating goat-loving piece of cattle muck."

His mom squeezed his shoulder. "What about you, Tyler, truth or dare?"

"You can't handle the truth."

When they laughed this time, the light dipped out.

"Oh, shit." He could hear his mom shaking it. "It's dead, or almost. Maybe I should turn it off awhile. I dare all of us to keep walking."

It wasn't so difficult. The light had been sporadic, more of a half promise than a dark-defying beam. He'd been so fixed on it that he'd forgotten the black blood that now pulsed around them. Without the light, everything grew louder. Their shoes crunched and he could feel his ears and eyes straining. Even his skin seemed to be pulling toward some point of contact. He stretched his arms out. Nothing. He raised them in front. He felt someone's shirt and gripped it between his thumb and index finger. The pressure of the black eased up, almost a sigh. He kept his eyes glued on where he imagined his feet were. The darkness didn't seem so loud as when he looked up and his ears pricked like a cat's and from behind them he heard the whispering, slithering motion of the cave.

"Do you see what I see?"

He looked up from the feeble beam tracing the floor in front of him. He'd been wondering what category a hurricane would have to be to reach Kentucky. He'd watched with Grandmom as the people in New Orleans waved white shirts at helicopters while the water poured over the levees. He'd built a levee in his cereal bowl, out of soggy corn flakes, then added milk and watched it find the weak spot. And there always was one. People talked about death and disease and still they wanted to go back home. And then Rita came. Some said the hurricanes were a warning from God, and someone talked about corruption at the local and state level, or it could be that monster storms were the wave of the future. He could see the map from the weather channel, with the red line pivoting from a central eye and behind it the green splash of bad weather. He could see the eye of the hurricane as it spun over the same tongue of southern Florida, and the next day, spinning again, only a little further along. Category 3, 4, 5.

"Is that daylight?"

He rubbed his eyes. Maybe he'd gotten turned around, but no, their voices were still in front of him.

"I don't see anything, Diana. Where do you see daylight?"

She didn't answer right away.

"Are you okay?"

"Apparently not. I was sure. I had my head down and I looked up and there was a kind of fuzzy square of light."

"Maybe it was lightning. Or maybe it's cloudy so we can't see it now. Let's keep going."

Maybe it was like a star that disappeared the longer you stared at it. You only saw it again if you looked close by. His legs trembled. They were on fire, the part that had gotten wet.

It happened to all of them at the same time. They were tired of holding their arms in front of them and had let them drop. Diana and his mother took the hit full in the face, and he followed, the impact softened by an arm, though he didn't know whose.

They were swearing, each of them bent over. He stretched his hands out until he felt the tops of their heads. He stroked them, Diana's yellow hair, spiky with the orange streak, and his mother's, long and smooth. Both gritty. He squatted and ran his fingers across Diana's face. It was wet, though she didn't seem to be crying. He lifted his hands again to see what they'd hit. Cool to the touch and rough, the steel beam stretched above his head and as far to each side as he could reach.

"I've got a feeling we're not in Kansas anymore. There's no place like home. Mama said life is like a box of chocolates—you never know what you're going to get."

"Okay, Tyler, that's enough." He could tell from her voice that she was trying not to cry.

"This is another nice mess you've gotten me into."

"I mean it. This is serious."

"Carpe diem. Seize the day, boys. Make your lives extraordinary."

"Tyler!"

"Somebody stop me!"

The back of her hand caught him on the chin and he stumbled into Diana, who grabbed his leg, the wet part, and then let go.

"Hasta la vista, baby."

It was easy to run back the way they'd come. He knew the way, because another eye, able to penetrate the ink, hovered in the air in front of him, guiding him around the bumps and holes in the floor. Behind him his name tapped against the back of his head, and her last words, "You'll be back. You've got no place to go."

Frankly, my dear, I don't give a damn, he thought. His knuckles slapped against the side of a wall and he slowed down. He wasn't in the middle of the shaft as he'd thought, but about to run into the wall. He took a deep breath. The stale air in this part of the tunnel was air he'd already breathed. It was air that knew him, or that he knew, having tasted it. This thought pleased him, and he sank to the floor, his knees drawn up to his chest, his hands pressed together between his legs. He was also, at the same time, breathing air that Diana had breathed, and his mother. Of course, this happened every day when you lived with someone, but it hadn't struck him till now that it was, in a way, like dreaming the same dream. Like *déjà vu.* He strained his ears to hear past the silence to what they might have said when they passed here the first time. Was this where Diana had said, "Did you ever get high with your husband?" He listened hard and thought that yes, he could hear a murmur, a trace of the conversation lingering, snagged by the greasy walls. She'd thought he was asleep.

"Of course, I did. I was an addict. But I got out. Having Tyler forced me out."

"Did you get pregnant and just quit?"

"Not right away. He used to cry all the time. About drove me nuts. I went to live with my Gram, and she used to hold him for hours. She just took out her hearing aids and rocked him, and eventually he'd fall asleep or eat or be still. I cleaned up on my own for a while, but then got into it again with Tyler's dad. When Tyler was about five, she told me her and my aunt would take care of him. I didn't know what she meant, but the next day, the police came and picked me up. Long story short, I was committed. I went to a place in Louisville. Ten Broeck."

"You're kidding. My sister went there too."

"Yeah? When was that? I was there in '99."

"Did you know Cecily Collins?"

"Jesus. You have to be shitting me. That's your sister?"

"You knew her? You're *that* Edna?"

So what. So someone's sister meets someone's mother in a crazy house, and then later that someone and the mother meet up in a mine shaft. Stranger things happen every single day. Like watching his dad look up from licking a plate and say, "Whose kid is that?" Like listening to his dad screwing some girl in the back of the truck, while he fiddled with the radio dial to drown out the slurring words, "Whatcha wanna spoil it for with one of those," and "Take me there, baby." Like standing on the side of the road after his dad kicked him out of the truck for backtalk and watching the taillights fade. Like walking for three hours till he got home and saw the truck parked in the driveway, then hearing his dad snoring and climbing upstairs to his room and into his bed, his legs so tired they vibrated, and his cat crawling over them and settling against his chest. She licked his hand and then his arm, and when a tear rolled down his cheek, she crept up and touched his face with her paw. He'd flung her away, but she came right back. He felt her throat with his fingertips and the rumbling peaked, then quieted to a mumble.

So what. It didn't mean anything. Walking home that night he went over and over it, what he'd said that was so bad as to cause his dad to make him walk home at two in the morning. They'd gone to someone's big house outside Harlan, someone who was running for sheriff. Some dare-a-lick from Texas with big cowboy boots caught Tyler by the arm as he was walking past and pulled him between his legs. "I'll give you $5,000 for this."

"He's worth twice that."

In the truck he'd said, "You spent more'n that on this piece of shit, and it don't even do your dirty work for you."

Smack. "If that's all the respect you got to show your father you can walk home and think about all I done for you."

A few cars passed. After the first one slowed down, he started hiding in the weeds whenever he heard the whine of tires. He didn't want to run into that Texan out here. Crouched there he watched a car full of partiers go off the road then get back on. A weak moon shed enough light to lay a ribbon through the trees where the road was. Coyotes on all sides yipped and howled. An owl cut a shadow across the sky. Crawling things rustled the leaves around him and from far away a dog's bark became a yelp and then silence. He could live with the animals, he thought, someplace like where his dad's strange uncle lived deep in the holler. Uncle Newby was crazy and everyone made fun of his hillbilly ways. Pipe. Piss can. Fishing pole. Green and blue bottles hanging from the trees. His mom used to say how living up there was just fine till someone broke a leg or got their foot caught in a trap.

So what. Accidents happen all the time, beginning with how you happen to get this mother and father. No one planned that. Not even God knew. So what if everyone went to church and said one thing and went home and did another. It wasn't good or bad.

So what if his daddy died in jail.

So what.

He'd fallen asleep but awoke when something flashed against his eyelids. He opened his eyes and waited. He could hear footsteps. Then another flash. Then silence.

"Are you there, Tyler?"

He held his breath. Another flash, this time closer. More silence.

Then, "Ah, there you are. I've got your picture here. Do you want to see?"

Her hand brushed the top of his head as she sank down beside him. She held the camera toward him and it lit up, showing a small square where his face rose out of a brown background, with Gollum's eyes.

"I told your mom I'd come find you. She's got a bad headache. She really bashed her head when we ran into that wall, that's why she didn't come herself. She's worried about you."

He wanted to say, "A boy's best friend is his mother," from *Psycho,* but his voice croaked, so he stopped. She lifted her arm and laid it over his shoulder.

"Is it okay if I do that? I'm kind of cold and you're warm."

He nodded and pressed his legs together so she wouldn't smell the piss on his pants.

"I think you've had a hard life for a little kid. You shouldn't be worrying about how the adults in your life are going to survive. You should be playing with kids your age, maybe be on a baseball team or something. Or maybe, seeing as you're smarter than the average bear, maybe on an academic team. Do they have those at your school?

"You know I lost my dad when I was twelve, not much older than you. He got killed in a car wreck. My mom took it hard so I felt like I had to take care of my two little sisters, you know? Kind of like something else bad would happen. When you're in the middle of something it feels like it's never going to end. But you know what? My baby sister is like elastic. She snapped back and put her great big heart into her horses. She's going to be a vet someday. My other sister took it harder. She got into a lot of trouble and did a lot of damage to, well, to everyone she knew, especially her family. Cuz it's your family that's easiest to hurt. You love them most and you hurt them most. Kind of funny, don't you think? Kind of backwards. Your mom was in the same place my sister was and your mom helped her, and I'm grateful for that, because, you know, my sister's my best friend. And she's doing okay now. Like your mom. Turning her life around.

"So I just thought you might like to know that everybody's got a story. Your story belongs to you, but it's also part of your mom's and your dad's story. And I sort of wondered what you thought of that."

Was she asking him to answer? He thought for a while, but nothing came to him.

"You talkin' to me?"

"Now, don't pull that one on me. I already heard you say that earlier."

"You don't understand! I coulda had class. I coulda been a contender. I could've been somebody, instead of a bum, which is what I am." Like Razzo Rizzo pissing himself on the bus.

"You're not a bum. Have you seen the movie *Little Man Tate?* You remind me of that kid a little. He was a genius. It was hard for him to fit in. And another similarity, you know, is that his mother loved him a whole lot, like your mom does."

"Oh good, that makes me feel so much better."

"I think you're being sarcastic, but I'm going to pretend you mean it. I'm sure that's from a movie. Maybe it's a good thing, since you've got such a good memory and have seen so many movies, so you can still express yourself, but it seems like a bad thing, too. Yes?"

"I'm fuzzy on the whole good/bad thing. What do you mean, 'bad'?"

"God, you're good. What's that from, can you tell me the name of the movie at least?"

"Ghostbusters."

"Ah. Well, okay, then, what's bad about it? If I swear that it will never leave this mine, will you tell me?"

It was tempting to stop rifling through the files in his brain, where the movies lined up like books on a library shelf. And here was Diana with the yellow hair and orange streak and she didn't know that most of the lines he used were ones he'd already used, over and over. They sounded new to her, so she thought he was clever, but they were old and tired. *It's bad to have people living in your head and telling you what to say. Sometimes their voices get so loud that they don't let you sleep, and sometimes it's hard to remember what you meant to say because what they're saying is not it at all. It's like breathing stale air. The words are someone else's air and you're speaking it.* But he didn't say this, and she didn't ask any more. When she stood up, she pulled him up, and they walked back to where his mother lay on her side.

He sat down in front of her and put his hand over hers, where it rested on her forehead. She whispered something and wiggled her little finger against his. His hand was warm and steady against the trembling iciness of hers. No one spoke and eventually she and Diana fell asleep. He listened to them rebreathing the air for a long time, as he practiced opening and closing his eyes. In his dream, he heard his granddad calling their names, and three strong beams of light swept over them. The three of them wept as they stood and hugged their rescuers. His legs no longer hurt, as if the rash had dissolved. In his dream they stepped out of the mine and into a late afternoon sunset with orange that streaked across a yellow sky. The sun itself was a great red balloon on a string that someone on the other side of the world was tugging down. He woke to the sound of someone saying: "They're coming. They're coming. I can see them coming."

On the Beautiful O-Hi-O

Married, Pat Likens lay in bed after her husband fell asleep, imagining his death. Now, after many nights of wrestling with insomnia, the visions had over-reached her, and she often fell asleep with tears in her eyes, as she slid into the second level of sleep, where consciousness floated on top like an anchored dock at the edge of a country pond. She could see the image and simultaneously feel herself a part of it, could see where she stood on the bank, just a few feet from two men fishing. Could feel the tugs on the end of her own line. Swinging her pole to the left and then to the right, steadily lifting it over her head as she coaxed it in, she felt elation creep like hot rum beneath her ribs.

She almost called out to the men, "I've got one!" but the dream took a turn. The fight intensified. Her shoulders strained and her feet slid in the muddy grass toward the pond. The pole bent dangerously, and suddenly the line angled beneath the bank, as though she were on a boat and the fish about to surface behind her. She even turned, and yes there were the trees, her car parked at the top of the small hill, the lawn chair with her book unopened in the grass beside it. She turned back and caught her first glimpse of something below the surface, and then her pole snapped. A moment later a man's arm grabbed hold of a root just inches from her foot and began to pull a body tangled in fish line out of the water.

She tried to sit up. In the early morning light that edged through a crack in the curtain she saw her husband's arm thrown over her chest. She could just make out at the roots of the black hairs, tiny flecks of mud or moss, and moisture seeping out. "Ugh," she groaned and lifted his arm. Her husband rolled over but did not awaken when she got up. She stepped into the shower and turned on the hot water, changed her mind and left it cold. Water beat in her face and the images of the dream sloughed off like rotted matter, leaving her breathless.

Later that morning as she prepared breakfast, the dream seemed foolish, even amusing. Her husband Carl came in rolling his sleeves up, as he always did on his way to work. As a programming consultant for a corporate insurance holding company, he traveled frequently. He kissed her on the cheek and said, "Morning! You sleep okay? I woke up and you weren't there."

"I got up to shower."

"Well, I don't like waking up alone."

"A big man like you." She loaded a panful of eggs on a plate and set them in front of him.

"Yeah, a big man like me. I like to wake up first, that's all. Same as you like to put mayonnaise on the bread instead of the meat. Don't need a reason."

She looked at him as he opened the morning paper and pulled his cup of coffee toward himself: his broad forehead furrowed as he read, his gray eyes slightly squinting. Was it honesty they held, as she had always thought? He wasn't at all bad to look at, but beneath that first skin—such weakness! The thought made her squirm, so she went over to the sink and began sorting through the supper dishes. After all, everyone's limited some way or another, right?

"Patina . . . Listen to this. . . ."

That name. Lately whenever he called her that, or worse, Patty-whack, her spine stiffened. She grimaced. How could she tell him that the name he had used for four years no longer suited? He was saying, "Oh, and this is what he says back to her . . ."

She tried to listen, but his voice sank into background noise that made washing dishes a pleasant, lulling activity.

When he left, patting her on the back and kissing her neck, she continued to feel disjointed and uneasy, and when she arrived in her own office, she decided to play a CD by Stephen Reich, which one of her students had given her, assuring her she could forget anything if she'd listen to it. She hoped the redundancy of the spiraling music would provide her with a rolling momentum that would allow her to coast through the papers she had to grade, but she stared at the pages and could think of nothing to say. She cleared her throat and settled down, letting a corner of her mind lift stock phrases from a large reservoir and guide her hand. She watched her firm knuckles dribble comments across the margins. "Can you explain this?" "Back it up!" Even an "Awk" or two slipped in. She couldn't have said what the writing was about.

Finally, she was down to the yellow half-way flap of the Notz-It she'd inserted as a reward. No one had stopped by. Nothing had impeded her progress. When she lifted her eyes after the last essay, the room spun right along with the strings, which were accelerating toward an apex, only in reverse, like water swirling toward a drain. The chair of the department, Hamilton Spears, walked in. The Chilean Chair, as her caver friend Meredith called him, the man with two last names, had a friendly, easy laugh and dark mischievous Spanish eyes. Whenever she was in the same room with him, she felt an unexplainable eagerness come over her and she imagined herself rushing over to him and hugging him joyfully.

"Morning, Likens! Didn't know you were a minimalist."

"I'm not," she said and flipped the player off. "But somehow it's gotten me halfway through a big set of essays."

His chuckle made her want to do something foolish, to make him laugh again.

"I'm not sure what my comments will look like," she said and lifted the edges of one paper. "Here, for example, the student has said—she's writing about her first baby's cesarian birth—'I realized then that it would not be a virginal birth.'"

When he laughed this time, he slid into the chair on the other side of her desk and crossed his leg. "And what did you say to that?"

"'Just say no.'"

"Works every time."

They began talking about department business and their voices turned thin and official—except once when she leaned toward him, and her voice seemed deep and guttural to her. She decided it would be best if she spoke as little as possible. Did he notice? When he left, she thought of reasons to follow him into his office. Perhaps she could talk to him about the student who wanted to bring his pet wolf into class or ask him if he'd read any good books lately. "What nonsense," she said out loud and stood up.

In Java City, located on the ground level of the library, she saw Meredith in line looking mean and grumpy. Pat gave her a hug and said, "You look beautiful this morning."

"Thanks. I needed that. I don't think I could stand more than another week of this. You going to the Jernigans' party next Saturday? Time to drink heavily. Maybe take a dip in the beautiful O-hi-o."

"Never. . . . Swim in the Ohio, I mean."

"Did you see this year's invitation?" Meredith flashed a sheet of shimmery paper in her face and Pat stared at herself peeking out of a mirror behind pink letters that declared the celebration to come. She drew back.

"What's the date?" she asked.

"The 24th."

"That's great."

"Why is it great?"

She started to say, "Because Carl will be out of town," but was unable to tell this to Meredith, who would have no patience with her staying in a relationship she'd surely consider dead.

Meredith peered at her, and Pat thought how similar her eyes were to the little flashlight doctors use to peer into orifices. "You look a little green around the edges," Meredith said.

"I guess I'd better get back in my pond. Oh, by the way, one of my students submitted a story that sounds a lot like you. I'd like to show you."

"Sure thing. You've got me curious now."

Meredith didn't ruffle the way Pat did, who was ashamed that she was forever doing what she should do, what was best for everyone concerned. She admired Meredith's calm assurance. When she was applying to school, for instance, she so resisted having to take the GRE in Geography that she had simply darkened one little circle per item and finished in fifteen minutes. "I refuse to do something that so misrepresents what I know," she'd said. The results had been so bad she had to retake it, but still, there was the satisfaction of saying no.

Pat watched Meredith's long straight back as she left the room and almost called out to her to come back, maybe get together for lunch, talk.

That night as she inhaled the musk that Carl always dabbed lightly on each hipbone and on his chest, she reveled in the muscles rippling beneath his skin, remembering an intimacy that hadn't been apparent to her for a long time. As he gathered himself above her, she slid her hand down his rump and pressed her finger into his anus. He clutched her and groaned as his full weight fell against her.

He lifted himself. "Where'd you learn that?" His words iced across her face.

"Just now is where."

"Seemed like you knew what you were doing and you haven't ever done that before—least not with me."

She tried to get up, but he held her down. "I'm not accusing you."

"Maybe you should."

He gripped her jaw. "Don't threaten me. I told you I can stand anything but that."

She held up his fist. "Don't you threaten me with this," she said and pushed his hand back into his own face. When she twisted from beneath him, he didn't try to stop her. She didn't turn on the light in the bathroom but stepped into the isolation of the shower and let the roaring of the shower head muffle her tears. Hot water washed over her, and when he climbed in and lifted her, separating her legs, she pushed him away. He had nicknamed them "sexy showers," and they had been erotic and ended in laughter. This time she turned from him and began soaping herself. He stood behind her for a moment then climbed out. "We okay?" he asked.

After easing herself back under the covers, she stared at the light of the moon as it passed slowly through the branches of their big oak. The digital clock said only an hour had passed. She closed her eyes and watched herself climb into a red sports car, taking the keys from him as he laughed at her, "But you don't even like to drive." She turned the handle that lowered the roof and said, "That's what you think!" saucy as the dickens. The air slipped around their sides and over their heads, creating a torrent behind them in the back seat. Her hair stung her eyes and cheeks, but she did nothing to pull it back. She asked him to look at the map for her, and with his head bent and trusting, she loosened her seatbelt, pushed her seat back, and as the car headed over a cliff, threw herself out. But she misjudged her leap and instead of landing safely near the edge, she rolled after the car and fell into space, head over heels, just like the car, wheel over wheel. She saw him reaching for her from the passenger's seat and she reached back, but they were too far away, and so they tumbled separately as the air sizzled around her. A moment later she stood on the cliff's edge watching as the car settled into itself in a cloud of dust and fire at the base of a tree.

In the morning she remembered the dream with dread. If she was going to break it off, she ought to hurry up and do it. The longer she waited the more painful it would be. She knew that. On the other hand, perhaps she was too critical, too demanding. What did she expect out of him, after all? She helped him pack with trembling hands. She could feel him watching her.

For weeks now he had tried to reclaim their old tenderness, and she had pulled back—going deeper into herself—or looked for ways to be with him just this once, to reach as he reached for that old thing, that something they'd lost the name for. She gritted her teeth and groaned, and when he misheard passion and excitement, she said to herself, "Okay, he could be anyone, so let him be anyone." A stranger. A sailor. Someone from work. A Greek god—Zeus, and she the swan who spreads her downy wings, her long neck turning gracefully as she flies away, while he looks up, caught at last in his human form. Lathered and musky he became an essence that she could drink.

Overwhelmed with sadness, she stopped in the middle of her packing and went to him, and when she took his face tenderly in her hands, his eyes misted. She kissed his lips then and pulled her body as close to his as she could, touching him with her arms, her breasts, her stomach, her thighs, her ankles. "Take care, baby," she said, "Get all the bugs out quickly and come on home. Maybe we can talk about our vacation. Huh? What do you say?"

"Sounds okay." She could feel his erection against her hip. "Are you going to see anybody while I'm gone?"

Her heart sank. He saw it in her face. "I didn't mean anything. Just a simple question. Out of curiosity. Talk about suspicious!"

They smoothed things over, but the tender mood was gone, and he left quickly. As she watched the car disappear down the road, her heart lifted.

Meredith was waiting for her, a latte at her lips, as Pat walked in. "Hey, come here!"

"What's up? Did you see that sun shining and those daffodils out front? It's spring!"

"Yeah, I don't think I can stand to teach today, but it's almost over and we're finishing up with the extremophiles, and they're more fun than daffodils." She gazed into the foamy coffee, her brow furrowed. "Well, maybe it's a tie. Anyway, have you heard? It looks like your Chilean Chair is moving on. I just heard some of your colleagues from History talking about it."

Pat's heart stopped beating for a moment.

"Why didn't he tell us first?" she asked. She felt a sudden anger at him for leaving, at Carl for failing her, at Meredith for finding out first. She snapped, "We get the announcement along with everyone else on this bloody campus. Who are we, his literary pimps? Why the hell is he leaving anyway?"

Meredith laughed. "Yeah, who does he think he is, anyway!"

"Good morning," his voice interrupted, as he pulled a chair to their table.

He smiled sheepishly. "I meant to tell you, but when I had to cancel our department meeting yesterday, I lost the chance, and the dean's memo had already gone out. I'm sorry."

Meredith said, "We didn't think you'd stand it as long as you did!"

Pat looked away. He glanced at her and said, "How's my number one literary pimp?"

She smiled, then mumbled, "I've got work to do," and rose quickly. In her own office, she closed her door and cursed as tears burned in her eyes. When someone knocked, she thought, *maybe it's a student,* though she knew better. She saw the doorknob turn and the tip of Hamilton's head. He leaned in further, keeping his eyes on the floor.

"Oh, come on. You're halfway in already."

He closed the door behind him and sat down. "Of all the people I work with," he started, "you're the one . . . "

"I'm the one. I'm the one."

He looked so good sitting in her chair like that, sheepish and apologetic, a little nervous, that she could easily imagine herself on her knees in front of him, her face buried in his lap, their arms entwined as he pulled her up. It seemed like such a good idea that she shifted her legs under her chair, pinning it down.

Her voice shook, "You have a good smile."

"So do you."

"You're just saying that."

"You're right. I am just saying it."

"Because I said it about you first."

"What—and it can't be true more than once every five minutes?"

"Never mind. I don't know why I'm like this. I'm glad for you and all that. It's just that I always miss people I get to know."

"Yes."

She began straightening piles of paper and tried to stop herself.

He said, "I'm forty-three and I want to go back out west where I grew up." He spoke slowly as though he wanted to make something very clear to someone unlikely to understand.

"You grew up out west?"

"Yes. Wyoming. On a ranch."

"You didn't grow up in Chile?"

"No, I wasn't even born in Chile, and I've only visited once."

"Is that why you don't have a name like Umberto or Rodriguez?"

He laughed. "You're showing your cultural limitations. But yes. I was adopted by my parents' employers when they died in a traffic accident. I was born on my mother's last breaths. They gave me each of their last names, Hamilton and Spears."

"I didn't know."

"It doesn't usually come up."

She didn't know how to respond. "Did you have horses?"

"A lot of horses."

"Will you have another one when you move out there?"

"I think two. For when company comes."

"Is that an invitation?"

"If you're passing through."

"Right. Wyoming."

He looked at his watch. "You've been farther. I have to get. We'll talk again?"

She didn't see him the rest of the day though he stayed on her mind. At home she ate a sandwich for supper and puttered around the house, cleaning slowly. At 9:00 she turned on a tearjerker and took pleasure in weeping as loudly as she could. At 2:15 she was still awake. She went to the medicine cabinet and took out a bottle of valiums and swallowed one. She couldn't stop thinking about Hamilton. She saw his crinkling brown eyes and his wide smile with the straight little teeth with a space in the middle. She could hear his laughter in her ear. She could even see them lying side by side, telling each other stories they had heard or made up as they breathed each other's breath. She could feel him inside her.

Intimates of the soul, she thought.

A dog barked. Another joined. Then the sharp, staccato notes lengthened and rose, climbing the cool night air as the dogs lifted their noses and howled to the full moon. How she had gotten lost, naked, in these big woods, she couldn't remember. But she found she could run fast and low to the ground without disturbing even a twig on a bush or a leaf beneath her feet. She lifted her head and sniffed. In the distance, the dogs had turned and begun their pursuit of her. Somehow, she knew that up ahead a cave offered shelter. If only she could reach it before they reached her. She looked around a moment longer, sensing which direction she should take. Her eyes picked out a rabbit a few feet away. Outlined in white, its eyes red, it stared at her. She could smell the presence of another, bigger animal, a new smell, one she couldn't place. It worried her more than the baying of the wild dogs, which grew louder as she paused. She turned and ran, the knuckles of her hands low to the ground, brushing the vegetation.

She began to climb. Ahead she saw the darkened entrance to the cave and behind her she felt the dogs' breath on her heels. Time paused as she slid into a weird space and an ethereal sound arose from the depth of the cave before her; she stretched her arms toward it and with a snap, her dream picked up where it had left. Her heart leapt to her throat when she saw him standing at the entrance, backlit by a fire. A bear? A man? His warm musk reached her stomach, and she bit her lip as the first dog leapt, its fangs bared and aimed for her throat. Moments later she rose, spectral, and watched as they devoured the white material body at her feet. She floated to the cave's entrance. When he saw her, now clearly just a man, he grabbed a club that lay near the fire. She was wary. She knew he was strong. She rose, sending her canine body around to the left while she slipped behind him. As he raised the club to bring it down on the dog, she wrapped her hands around his neck and squeezed.

As he slumped to her feet, she opened her eyes. It was morning, quite late it seemed, for the sun was shining brightly into the room. She stumbled to the bathroom and looked into the mirror, saw her sunken eyes and swollen lip where she had bitten it in her sleep.

Given the hour's drive before her, she had decided not to go to the party, not to expose herself to the superficial talk, the inevitable fluttering over Hamilton that she knew would be forthcoming, the slurred chatter of her colleagues. But the house seemed both claustrophobic and empty at once. She needed to get out. She had napped again in the late afternoon, a blissful, dreamless sleep, and felt ready for the company of others. The phone rang as she slid into a loose knit dress that touched her only at the shoulders.

"Hi, Patina!"

"How's it going?"

"The programmers here need to go back to the school. A lot of stupid mistakes. There's one who's good and she's a big help. Turns out she was at Duke when we were, and here she turns up in St. Louis. Small world. You'd like her. She's smart. Even reminds me of you."

Why was he telling her all this? To make her jealous? She could imagine him in bed with someone like herself. He would be gentle and solicitous, then a little bit brutal, perhaps, overcome by desire, and she would feel overcome by it, and the two would go at it like gangbusters and later drift off to sleep thinking they had achieved something.

When she arrived at the party, the main rooms were already crowded. She worked her way to where she knew the drinks were being served, stopping to chat every so often, usually about the weather or the end of the term or the resignation of Hamilton Spears. Such a good name for him, really. Unexpected. Two strong last names. Two nationalities: one blood, one legal. She saw Meredith waving at her from the stairs. She stood with Hamilton—he had his back to her but turned when he saw Meredith waving. Pat gestured to the bar and they nodded.

She asked for two drinks, preferring to have the ice melt in the second than to weave her way through this mess again. She looked back toward Meredith and Hamilton but could only make out the top of his head. Too many people to struggle against. She slipped out the patio door and headed with long strides toward the river so people would think she was meeting someone—it would explain why she was carrying two drinks. No one stopped her. It was as though she weren't even there. She walked in the shadows of the trees, then slipped through a break in the hedge. On the other side of a path the grass sloped steeply toward the river. She knew that on at least one occasion the river had risen beyond the hedges and had lapped into the house, causing more bother than financial setback. That had been about five years ago, the worst flood of the century, not expected to happen again.

She walked down the hill on the sides of her feet and when she reached the bottom, she stood on a grassy bank. A bench looked precarious but didn't move when she tried to rock it. Such an odd angle, almost as though it had been washed up to the shore, though she thought that ridiculous since it was concrete and probably too heavy to be borne, even by the Ohio. Perhaps it had rolled down here in the flood, and they had never bothered to carry it back up, buying new lawn furniture instead and letting this stay put. Perhaps Billy Jernigan or even his prissy wife came down on occasion to listen to the river lap at their feet.

She drank the first drink quickly and flung the ice cubes into the water. Across the river the hills were dark except for a small cluster of lights. When she trained her eyes on the distant lights, the river itself seemed to define itself in terms of conflicting currents and eddies that she hadn't perceived before. It wasn't so dark here as it had been in the backyard where trees blocked the moon's light. In fact, she noticed the moon just rising above the line of trees to her right. As it emerged from the last tangle of branches, the water caught its yellow reflection and unfurled it smooth as silk. The Ohio had always seemed treacherous to her but now it was beautiful, beguiling. When she looked closer at the water near her feet, she could see the murky depths churning with motives of their own. She jumped when someone's hand rested on her shoulder.

"Sorry. I didn't mean to scare you."

"It's okay," she said, and sipped from her second drink, tucking it into the empty cup. Hamilton continued to stand beside the bench, looking out at the river.

"It's pretty tonight," he said. "May I sit?"

"Yes. Pretty and deceptive." As he stepped in front of her, he looked back up the hill toward the house. "I don't know why more people aren't down here."

"I guess it just hasn't occurred to them. After all, it's a party at the Jernigans' and that means you eat and drink and sit on their expensive furniture and look at their original art."

"You sound a little cynical. Isn't some of that art by Meredith's mother?"

"Yes, but I just don't understand why they couldn't have gotten a big house on the Barren River and save us the drive." She looked away from him but felt him glance at her then turn back to the river.

"Where's Carl tonight?"

"St. Louis. I don't want to talk about him."

He was silent. They looked at the river and she listened to it licking at the shore, sending tiny waves from out of its vast belly. A tugboat emerged, its loan light inconsequential in the moon's strong glow. She hadn't noticed the barge in front of it until this pinpoint of light emerged pushing it. Had they been only looking in the direction of the river, sensing the swelling and turning of the currents beneath and missing the activity of the surface? She wanted to take his hand, and now that he was leaving, why not? What did she have to lose? She wouldn't have to face him the next day at work. He no longer even worked with her anymore. She reached across the space between them and took his hand from his lap and brought it over to her own. He continued to look out across the water. His hand surprised her. So different from

Carl's thick, muscular hands; she could feel through the skin to the interlocking bones. They seemed inexplicably lovely to her. He responded to the pressure of her fingers, tightening his own.

"I will miss you," she said, "I didn't know until I heard you were leaving that I would."

He sighed. "Pat," he said.

Had she ever heard her name spoken like that? So sweet and full of something tender, not to be touched. Had he really said it? It seemed as likely to have been the voice of the lapping waves speaking to the shore, over and over, "pat . . . pat" beneath the sound of the tug, beneath their own voices and thoughts, and now speaking despite the laughter of people approaching behind them. They turned to look. She thought they might withdraw their hands, but they stood up, still linked, and moved away.

Her heart raced. She didn't know how to prolong or to end the moment. They walked until a fallen tree stopped them, then headed back up the hill. When they had reached the corner of the house, their hands dropped.

"Here we are." He took a step toward the house then stopped when she didn't follow.

"I'm not going back in," she said. "I'm going home."

He looked at her then down then back to the house. He seemed unable to fix on anything.

"Good-night," she said quickly, "we'll talk again?"

"Yes, of course."

When she arrived home the phone was ringing. She answered it and Carl said, "Hey, honey, you just getting home? I been calling every half hour or so." He waited for her to answer. "I just wanted to tell you how much I love you and how much I miss you. How was the party?"

"Fine."

"Good. Did you talk to anyone?"

"No. Even though they were friendly and talked to me I refused to say a word."

"Ha. Ha. I know you're just teasing."

"I'm tired. It's late. Do you have anything else to say?" She tried to sound kind.

She replaced the receiver and crept up to bed. The moon shone brightly through the window, where she had failed to close the curtains. She lay on her side, watching it. Her husband and Hamilton and Meredith seemed to be rushing away from her into a dark night, where the only sound was of someone crying. But she did not feel sad as she lay curled in her own arms listening to the waves rocking against the wooden slats of an old rowboat tethered to a bush on the shore. In it she could see her husband gesturing for her to join him. She leaned down and loosened the rope and with her foot pushed the boat out. He gripped the sides. The boat moved swiftly into the current and soon she lost track of it as a barge bearing coal appeared out of the darkness to the right, its square little tugboat pushing it on with a winking light and a distant thrum.

Extremophiles

I'm a geologist. We think of time differently, where change cannot be tracked with the human eye, usually, though sometimes a cataclysm brings the underworld into the timeframe we recognize on earth. When he was forty-two, my husband David drove into a tree a quarter mile from home, leaving me with three daughters to raise. Even when lifting my head was as far above the surface I could reach, they were the terrain I couldn't ignore, no matter how hard, below, David was pressing against me.

My mother had given it to me the previous Christmas, the black journal with no lines, no page numbers, and two days after the accident, my fingers knocked against it as I rifled through his jeans drawer, forgetting what I was looking for, though I could see from the other open drawers with clothes spilling out that it had been something important. Here would be the line I fed into the darkness, where he had fallen to an unreachable depth. Every night I read it before bed, opened it to a page and let the suffering me out, so she could sleep. I have inserted pictures here and there, taking them from family albums, most of them, making copies so that the originals retain their place in our family history. Why is it that this journal records so much pain, when these pictures show so much laughter? Am I so morose as all that? Is it wrong to keep him tied to this darkness, this flickering light?

I suppose we all develop rituals. When I repel to a lower point in a cave, I pause a moment, turning to each of the four other directions. I bow my head, *bring me home safely.* It's dark, no one knows I do this. We all need a little bit of OCD so we don't spin away, so we can place ourselves here, where the past and future come together, in ritual. Even our horses turn a certain way in their stalls, sleep with their noses in the same corner, whicker one way when they're hungry, another way when they're tired. The girls are tucked in. The house is darkened. I light candles, stack pillows against the headboard, set the books beside me: the old journals, the new one with a pen inserted into the page where I might write, if I feel moved. I say his name, once. David. Let the journal fall open. Sometimes I write in my current journal, referring to an older one, #4, page 17, correcting things: *I must be remembering wrong. It wasn't until we were married and I was pregnant that I first knew something was wrong with you. There had to be. Overnight, you had changed, my heartbeat, became silent, withdrawing. I blamed myself, tried harder—sex, cooking, conversation—sure I could lift you out of this "particularly blue blue," as you used to call it, and rescue you from yourself.*

I'm sure there are other ways. Some people drive themselves into their work, numb the mind that way. I have done this, too, but the harder I pushed, the faster I saw him gaining on me, ready to cuff me in the back of the head, lay me out flat. No, I had to give him this space, every night. Even when I went to conferences, I didn't share my room, and I carried a candle and one of the journals with me.

For a while, before I could begin writing, I read everything I'd written previously, so there was no doubt where I'd been, mapping my way until I'd written so much I fell asleep without uncapping my pen. These first pages, then, are the most worn. I know them by heart.

The end is the beginning of the end is the end of the beginning.
I don't remember much of the last two weeks. Dr. Keene insisted on valium because the back of my neck is a corkscrew catching my shoulder muscles and threatening to pull the entire fabric into a big knot. When I got out of bed it was to use the bathroom.
I don't understand what's happening. I know that David is gone but then I know he's not. I lie in bed staring into the space between the bed and the dresser until the dresser and bed disappear. Wings are beating in my head, at my eardrums, and though I call for help the words can't climb the barrier of my tongue, and so I crouch at the back of my throat and listen.
Under the beating he comes, close enough so I can sense him behind the great wings that make it impossible to move, even to call to him. But I can hear him call me. "Meredith!"

He sounds impatient. I try to answer. The wings slow and he slips away and finally evaporates into space, and then I am alone in the place where water flows uneasily over rocks that gradually rise above me, shadowing the light. Why can I hear him and he not hear me? This morning I called for Diana, and she answered right away as if she was there in bed with me.

How loyal she is. But there's a want in her that makes me turn away. I want to go back to bed. If I can climb onto the wings, I can maybe see him and reach him.

I chew the valium now to go down there.

It's been two weeks and now I'm writing down these thoughts, catching up. Why not, there's not a moment when you are not in my head, so I might as well tell you what your leaving has done to us. Last week, my first day out of bed since I went to it after the funeral, I woke up to her trembling voice. "Mom?"

I turned away from her, but her hand squeezing my shoulder insisted. "Mom?"

"Go see Grandma, Diana."

"Grandma sent me in here to bring you some dinner."

So, it wasn't morning, but evening.

Other hands. "Come on, Mommy, me and Diana brought you some soup we made."

"Who's that? Is that you, Molly?" I leaned against the pillows they had stacked behind me. "And where's Cecily?"

"She's outside somewheres."

"Somewhere, Molly, not somewheres." (Who cares! I had the presence of mind to think.)

"Somewhere."

"I think I'd like to get out of this old bed. It smells like old gym shorts."

Molly spoke solemnly, "Like Uncle Ned's socks."

Then, Diana, "I'll wash them for you. You go sit in the kitchen."

I sat on the edge of the bed with a drug hangover that had my hands shaking.

"Get her robe and slippers, Molly."

Molly bent over to slide the slip-ons onto my feet. Her striped t-shirt stretched over her narrow back, and her long braid dividing her back slid to the side. I grabbed it and filled my two hands with it, then put my face in it and breathed her in. Molly stood slowly.

"Who braided your hair so nice?"

"Cecily."

"She's done it just right, not so tight that it twists."

It was a small thing, but when Molly's face flushed and her chin quivered, I felt as if I'd been kicked in my stomach. Your chin has become Molly's! Have I only just now noticed, or has it become yours in the intervening days, jutting out with its longing for you?

They helped me into the hall. I asked them how long I'd been in bed.

"Since Friday. Since the funeral. Five days."

"And has Grandma been here the whole time? And Uncle Ned?"

This time Molly answered. "Grandma's staying in Cecily's room because she's acting funny, and Grandma says it's better she sleeps with her."

"Where's Cecily now?"

"Outside somewheres."

"How is she acting funny? Diana?"

"She's okay, Mom. She's not acting funny, Molly."

"I guess we're all acting funny, aren't we? Most of all your mother."

Now that I've seen my girls and know that they are suffering on my account, I have to make a better effort. I have to act like we're still a family and that they haven't lost us both.

(Thank you, Mom and Ned, for loving my girls and for letting me sleep in.)

I recorded conversations back then for David, imagining that he was listening, could read over my shoulder. After this last entry, I got the idea of inserting pictures, taping just along the top, so I could flip the picture up and read what was underneath. I inserted a picture over the last line that shows our family—our girls, Mom, Ned—David and I are outside the frame, of course. I took the picture, but I'm not there. Like David, I have left them to their own devices.

If you look at the second year, will you see that I am getting better? I don't see it, though I think maybe I held a grudge against David that began to show. I began to sense that I had given more of myself than I could afford. Was I wrong to tape a picture of my lover over this next passage? I look at his picture and can hardly remember the passion he had for me, bowling me over and making me forget how distant David had become. But at the time, he gave me something I needed. He folded me in his arms so tenderly.

I'm glad you never knew I once loved anyone else but you. David, maybe now you can forgive me, because I know you never would have when you were alive. You would have been hard on me. The year Sam was here was the year you wrote your first book, The Write Stuff. *That's all you cared about, clever exercises and witty sayings, notes everywhere, tacked up around your typewriter—just before we got our first computer. You invited your students to the house, your protégés, trying out your exercises on them. Snarling at me. Ignoring Diana and Cecily. Sam came after me in a big way and I fell into him. We loved a few months and then he had to leave, his appointment had been only a year. He called me a few times, but by then it was over. You had finally gone to the doctor, were trying meds for the first time, and most of all you had apologized. You held me when you cried that night when you started loving me again. I remember thinking, is this all I needed to stay true—you, my love?*

Certain memories keep coming to mind. Last week there was one, and this week two. I go over and over them, as if they hold an answer that I can hear but not interpret. When I was little our phone line let us hear other conversations in the distance, we could pick up laughter, raised voices, intonation, but they were too far away to understand. I'd press the phone to my ear, tell whoever I was talking to to hush, then try to pick up a word or two. Who were these people? There was always a woman who laughed a lot. I got closest to hearing her, the child's voice too high and the men's voices too low to pick up more than a rumble, like surf. Once she was crying and the other voice was angry. I wanted to say, "Let her alone, you bully," a sound if not words that would stop them cold, but they couldn't hear me the way I could hear them.

So, I'm listening to these snatches of memory for something underneath. Last week's: After one of my bladder infections, maybe the third that year, I was sitting on the toilet groaning as the burning made my jaw clench, and you came in. You ruffled my hair and said, "I feel bad that you're always the one to get sick. How about tonight you rub my penis till I get a bladder infection?" This made me laugh and a new drop of pee sent chills up to my teeth. "Don't flirt with me when I feel like this."

Then this week, it's just your arms around me as you used to do when you were feeling affectionate and would come up behind me, rest your chin on my head, and rock back and forth, until one of us broke away, or made it into something more. . . . David, my love, I sleep alone now, and always will. That's not just a sad song. I know it all the way to my bones.

The third memory is new. You're calling my name from the barn, where you've gone to work on something, and I'm exasperated to have to stop what I'm doing. When I get there, you say you didn't call. I don't remember this ever happening, but at the same time, it comes to me as something that happened long ago.

I was in the kitchen, slicing some cake for the girls yesterday, when this memory that never happened hit me again. I stared out the window at the barn. I could see your work boot then the cuff of your jeans, then the knee, your thigh, your right hand, and then you dissolved. I put the slices on plates and silently begged my girls to distract me. They did. Homework. A broken Snoopy lamp switch. *SNL* reruns.

Memories begin to sort into types. Specific events that I knew had really happened—some called up at will, others leaping out of a monotonous landscape of dulled feeling. Sensations—smells, heat, the weight of arms—hauntings that came and left unbidden, but slowed me down, sometimes to a standstill. Images that couldn't have been but which I remembered nonetheless, shooting him into the present and then disintegrating. Three evolutionary arms had developed, and I followed one, then the other, into darkness.

Last night at my grief counseling group, I told the story (again) of how you died, the suddenness, the violence, the senselessness of it. I said that while I know what our therapist has said, that making sense of random loss is not possible, I need an explanation that will lighten this ton of rocks I carry in my heart. It pulls my posture down in front and makes my back a shaft of barbed wire. It's over a year and there is NO lessening of the pain. I walk through the motions

*at work, at home, a crummy mother and a crummier teacher. I must
do better. But I can't wait till they're in bed and I can be alone with
my thoughts.*

*She told us that the second year is often harder than the first,
and that this surprises the grievers. And it surprises the watchers.
Why doesn't she get over it, they wonder. But she's right, this year is
worse in some ways because your absence has grown solid, definite.
I can trace the edges and feel the carved roughness of limestone,
here your shoulder, something I melted into, now cold and rigid. You
have become the cemetery marker you wanted no part of. Cast me
to the air, you told me, if I go before you. No marker, no funeral. I
honored your wishes, the funeral our own, no body, no casket, just
a roomful of pictures, your jeans and corduroy shirt draped over a
chair, as if you had just slipped them off.*

*I don't want you to grow harder and darker, to merge with
the landscape.*

After three years the journal stops suddenly—except for this
last entry, which I wrote last year: *I went to the national conference
last weekend and presented a paper on extremophiles. You used to
say, "You geographers are really closet poets, making up words and
telling stories. You're not scientists like other scientists." Snottite
was the girls' favorite term; yours, extremophile. You wrote a poem
about them, those tiny microbes who survive 176 degrees Fahrenheit,
even more, near the boiling point. I still remember the line, "living
beyond the edge / in the murky pot / of earth's bowels."*

I stopped writing so suddenly because my journal was discovered
by our housekeeper Mary. She read it, and she even used part of it
in a story she was writing for a class taught by one of my friends.
It shocked me, the idea of a stranger reading my most intimate
feelings. It was as if she had entered the ritual, uninvited, and I
could no longer perform the steps. I tried. Lit the candles, read
the entries, held the pen over the page, ready to trace what I had
felt that day. Nothing. I hadn't wanted to be overheard. But now
I wonder if she didn't save me, in a way.

For I have grown brazen, trumpeting my private thoughts for
a reading public, most of whom I'll never meet. Someone said,
"You seem to be making an industry out of loss." Once, I would

have carried that insult around like a bur under a saddle, allowing it to fester. But I understand. His office is across from mine, I'm a shifting plate in his landscape, and he prefers the familiar, in his colleagues, and in his work. It's not his to understand why I took to opening my private pain to a public gaze.

It began a few years ago, well after I stopped writing in the journals, when a colleague who is a lead researcher in the Lechuguilla Canyon near Carlsbad invited me to join her and a small team of explorers. I had been dropping hints, and now they wanted to invite a few geologists and microbiologists from elsewhere in the country to view for ourselves the most beautiful gypsum formations ever seen. Microbes in Carlsbad had fed on oil, producing hydrogen sulfide gas as part of their metabolism. This gas was released, mixed with oxygen, and formed sulfuric acid. Over time, the sulfuric acid ate the limestone, leaving the sparkling white gypsum formations. Now the cave is dead, the original healthy eaters long gone, but dead only means there's no new cave being formed by sulfuric acid. New microorganisms are eating the walls, creating rust patches that speak of life.

Getting there was hell. At the entrance, the wind blows up to 50 miles per hour, but once the door is slammed shut, it shudders to a murmur, then silence vaster than any I'd known rushes in. Caves don't just throw back voices in echoes, they listen. This cave was a great ear, and I could feel it pressing itself against my skin. I was terrified of plummeting hundreds of feet with a thin rope and a hand brake, all that kept me from a fall that could be as easily up as down, so suspended space had become.

We repelled down pit after pit, communicating in quick exchanges. "Okay, made it." "More line." "Careful." A rockslide below left me dangling for thirty minutes, and though I could hear the voices of others as they checked for damage and re-established the safety lines, they were far away, like traffic on a distant highway. In perfect darkness I waited, suspended in the great throat of the cave. My line turned me slowly and now I heard it. A breath, a low sigh, a loneliness so deep that it had lost the awareness of self that loneliness usually heightens. I reached my hand out and the sigh rose. My lips opened, and the sigh shot up from the depths.

Once on solid ground, a light flashed across my face, expressions of concern followed, a hug. I realized my face was wet with tears. I shifted quickly to the researcher they'd invited. I photographed everything, but especially the u-loop formations that colleagues had surmised were calcified snottites. Studying them in another cave, Villa Luz, in Mexico, they've deduced a similar life story for Lechuguilla. The mucus-like substance dripping from the snottites is stronger than battery acid, dissolving clothes and burning if you touch it. At Villa Luz, the walls of the new cave are alive with dripping acid, and yet living in its midst are communities of mites, worms, tiny bugs, spiders. Their environment is extreme only to us. Back in Villa's older sister cave, a mile in, we stopped and drank from Lake Labarge, a body of water so clear it might as well be air you drink. No one spoke. I pointed my flashlight at the water, saw the circle of light hover on the surface, then dive to the bottom. Air and water might have been the same substance.

I had gone to see a different cave formation than the ones I grew up with in Kentucky. I wanted to step outside of what had become home. I have been there three times now and co-written two papers trying to help untangle the mysteries that fascinate us. It happened in the midst of writing that second paper, the sudden certainty that I was telling only half the story—the surface of life beneath the surface—and so I began writing travel pieces for non-academic magazines, essays about life in all its extremities.

One day several months ago I ran into my old grief counselor, Shannon, who asked if I'd like to attend again. "Your experience will be beneficial," she said. After the fourth meeting, I invited them to my house. I led them into the living room, where light pours cheerfully (I thought) through the windows. I had pulled enough comfortable chairs for everyone into a circle. Donna had been in the group longest. Her son died in a traffic accident and wasn't discovered for two days. Always fragile but resolute, Donna made a beeline to my 300-pound geode. "That's a mighty big Easter egg," she said. I told her I'd always thought of it as an egg as well, though David called it "G"nome the Ge-ode. "David bought it for me on a trip out west, and our oldest daughter sat next to it in the backseat across the country, each of them strapped in. She described everything as we went, saying he was too short to see out the window. David was ready to throw it out the door by the time we hit Kansas."

Charlie walked up and looked over her shoulder but said nothing. Our newest member, he was grieving his wife of thirty years, who had died of cancer a year before. "I don't know how to be with people anymore," he said. Ida's and Karen's husbands died in the Iraq war, and they were angry and scared. Though they hadn't met before joining the group, they now seemed inseparable. Our last member, Parker, was a tall, gaunt man whose son had died of AIDS.

When Shannon called at the last minute to say her car had broken down, I felt a surge of uncertainty, which I tried to hide by getting busy with serving cookies and tea. Ida suggested we get started. I was surprised at how dependent we were on Shannon, so gifted in getting us to share, prompting now and then when we slipped into dangerous areas—denial, blame—though most of the time she just listened. Without her, what we were doing seemed artificial, and since it was my house, the superficiality was mine. What could a grief addict offer a small group of unhappy people except the assurance of more misery?

Suddenly, amid an uncomfortable silence, Charlie stood up and pointed. "There's a horse trotting by."

"There's another one!" cried Parker.

They jumped to the windows, as if they'd never seen horses before. I tried to tell them it was no big deal. "Babe knows how to open the paddock door. They like to see what's going on when we have company." I looked from one to the other, stunned, as their pretenses peeled away like extraneous skin. They didn't know they were being watched. Each one stood rapt, smiling, even Donna. Though she usually cried through meetings, her lips were lifted in a half-smile.

"Would you like to help me put them back?"

They practically ran to the door, and I followed them into the yard, where Babe and Iago were stepping among them, nuzzling their hands for treats.

"Hold on! I'll get some carrots," I called, turning back toward the house, but not before I saw Charlie run his hand appreciatively over Iago's shoulders. When I returned with the carrots, our other two horses had arrived, knowing that Babe would find treats if there were any. Donna had pressed her forehead against Hasbeen's face, and I could see her shoulders shaking.

After treats, we led the horses back to the barn and groomed them. I showed them which brushes to use, how to follow the direction of hair around the swirls at their hips and shoulders. They learned names—muzzle, withers, chestnut, cannon bone. Ida and Karen braided manes—individual braids, a French braid. Charlie and Parker worked the hooves, cleaning them with the hook.

"I used to have a horse," Parker said, "but I haven't been near one in thirty years."

It was evening when Donna, the last to go, finished sweeping the barn. She hugged me as I walked her to her car, a long hug, a hug I released her from twice and still she held on. When she finally pulled away, tears stood in her eyes. "You're blessed," she said.

Shannon has asked that I co-facilitate first one then another group. We meet in my living room then we go to the barn—and sometimes we meet in the barn. Sometimes, we ride, but touch is best, and so they groom the horses and feed them treats. We meet with a group of refugees from Bosnia, still blocked from expressing in a foreign land and a foreign tongue what they never needed to know about the depths of suffering. One woman originally from Korea cries and laughs simultaneously as equine lips nuzzle her open hand. "Oh, that tickle," she says. "But it feel so good."

Why do I tell you this? I don't know what work you do, where you teach or write or count or file. I am a geologist. I study caves. But I'm shifting, exposing new layers. A counselor, a writer—like David was, who sought in words the mysteries of the world.

Who have you lost? What betrayal chips away at your chance for happiness? I lost a husband. I came close to losing my middle daughter. She almost died twice, pushing herself as though by running toward danger she would evade it. Then one day she came to me. My head was full of work, but something in her face made me set it aside. You see, my tender-hearted daughter whose armor people have so often mistaken for coldness, came to tell me she had been on the floor behind the driver's seat when David died. He heard her move and reached back to touch her. Then he drove into the tree. For thirteen years she scraped herself against the certainty that she had killed him, despite avoiding it with all she had. She is a nurse now, working in the ER, helping others hold onto life. She says to me, after I let her read this, after I tell her it's hers, "Oh, let them have it, if they want it, it was mine for long enough."

I have a collection of rocks, labeled and lined up in neat rows. They lie in drawers that pull out for easier viewing. I have a new drawer now, where creatures who died in caves I visited are meticulously positioned. Some are too small to see, so I capture them with a microscope and photograph their startling shapes. I set these square photographs next to their 3-D cousins. You can see their tiny legs, their knock-kneed clumsiness, the spot where the eye would be if the eyes hadn't devolved thousands of years ago from lack of use. They are cave-colored, cave-determined, cave-creators. They remind me of the dark places where life goes on.

About the Author

Poet and writer Jane Olmsted is a retired professor of English and interdisciplinary studies at Western Kentucky University. Her poems and stories have appeared in *Nimrod, Poetry Northwest, The Beloit Fiction Journal, Adirondack Review,* and *Briar Cliff Review,* among others. A chapbook *Tree Forms* was published in 2011 (Finishing Line Press). Her essay "The Weight of a Human Heart" won *Memoir Journal's* prize for the guns issue, fall 2013. Her collection of poetry, *Seeking the Other Side,* was published by Fleur-de-lis Press in 2015 and a memoir, *The Tree You Come Home To,* was published in 2021 (Legacy Book Press).

Artist's Statement

I am a Kentuckian. My ancestors, for five generations, or more, have lived their lives in the remote hollows and the rocky slopes of south central Kentucky where they are buried in graveyards and homesteads lost to memory.

Floyd Collins is my grandmother's first cousin.

When Jane Olmsted shared with me her manuscript, *Letters from the Karst,* it was a revelation—so steeped it is in the land and the culture of my people I recognized it immediately, and I knew right away I had to illustrate the cover.

My choices for content, media and design were—I realized almost after the fact—inspired by the complicated and nuanced emotional responses Jane managed to evoke in me as I navigated her web of interconnected tales—not a roller coaster ride, exactly, but a winding trail, for sure—one that leads through bright sunshine and dark shadow.

Black ink wash seemed the perfect way to explore those gradations of light and dark, and I have always been drawn to traditional Asian black ink art, in part because it can capture flowing water in ways that other media cannot.

The waterfall itself is hidden in a remote corner of Warren County, Kentucky, that the locals (myself included) call Shanty Hollow. It cannot be found on a map.

Teresa Christmas